6/2017

FRA

Fallin' for

a Boss

By: Lucinda John

D1527991

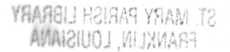

Dedication

Celina John, the woman that gave birth to me. Although you're no longer with us I just want to thank you. Thank you for giving me life and raising me to the best of your abilities. I love you so much and I wish you were here to watch me grow into the wonderful woman that I am becoming. I love you lady!!! R.I.P

To my babies Kamauri, Kaiden, and the little one growing in my womb. You guys are the reason I wake up each morning with ambition. Everything I do, I do for you three. Mommy loves y'all!

Acknowledgments

First I want to give all the praises to God. If it wasn't for you providing me with such a creative gift I wouldn't be able to write books. I look back on all the things I went through, all the times I cried and questioned my purpose and all along it was right here in the keys of my laptop. Thank you so much for everything that you do for me and I want to praise you in advance for all that you will do.

To my kids, you guys are my backbone, my reason, my purpose; I love y'all!!

Charles, I know I drove you crazy growing up, but thank you. Love you daddy.

Brian Mesidor, this been a crazy eight years. LOL! Thank you for everything you did for me and most importantly for my kids. You are a wonderful father and I will always love you.

Alette, Sylvie, Lines, C-way, Drew, and Alan we are Celina's angels. Even though we're not always around each other or talk every day I love y'all very much. Lynn,

Lelaine, Chentale, and Leonise. I love y'all very much for adopting me into your family and treating me so well.

Lurjie and Kerby my best friends, thank you for being there to listen to me. Cassie, Rose, Jojo, Syndy I love y'all! To all my friends and family that didn't mention, I ain't forget about you; I LOVE Y'ALL too!!!

Last but not least I would love to thank Myss Shan. Thank you for believing in me and for giving me such a great opportunity. Oh and to my Shan Presents family, all of you ladies are such wonderful people and I love you all dearly. SP4L!!!!!

Text Shan to 22828 to stay up to date with new releases, sneak peeks, and more from Shan and the ladies of Shan Presents

Chapter 1

James

The smell of bacon woke a nigga up to a growling
stomach. I must have put it on wifey good last night for her
to be up cooking a nigga breakfast. Getting out of bed, I
noticed that this was not the Versace Silk Satin sheets Lala
bought for two stacks last week Instead, I was laying on
the forty dollar Target sheets that belonged to my side
bitch.

SHIT!! I couldn't believe I allowed my ass to stay out
at this THOT's house for so long. I was sure that I set my
alarm to wake me up in four hours after I got here.
Speaking of my phone, where the fuck was it?

"Good morning daddy!!" Ashley walked into the room with a tray of food snapping me out of my thoughts. I ain't gon lie, the bitch did look good standing there in nothing but a thong and a fitted white tank top that showed off the belly ring that she got with my initials on it.

"Yo, where the fuck is my phone?" I replied not paying her or that food no mind. My main focus was coming up with a lie that I had to feed Lala and prayed that she fed into the bullshit I was about to give her ass.

"I turned it off and put it on the dresser," she answered putting the food down on the nightstand next to me.

"Bitch, who the fuck authorized yo' silly ass to touch my shit?" I yelled, jumping out of the bed and grabbing the bitch by her throat. I swear I wanted to strangle this bitch to death for being so damn dumb.

I threw the hoe on the ground and quickly grabbed my phone and powered it on. As soon as the phone turned on, notifications were coming in back to back. *Damn!* I was gonna be in some deep shit with wifey as soon as I got home. I mugged the hoe as her pathetic ass lay on the ground crying. I should stomp a mud hole in her ass for not knowing her place.

I quickly threw on my clothes, snatched my fitted cap, keys, and ran out that bitch's house without even closing the door. The ride back home was a forty-five minute drive.

"Fuck!" I yelled as a text message from wifey came in: *you can keep yo black ass where you slept last night.*

Chuckling, I picked up the phone to text her crazy ass back: *Bae just chill I'm omw home right now;* I replied hitting the send button.

Thirty minutes later, I pulled up to our house and parked my car behind Lala's apple red Lexus that I bought her last month for getting caught fucking with this stripper hoe. I pulled the blunt that I had pre rolled from my ashtray and lit that bitch. I had to get mad high before I went inside the house to deal with my ol' lady's wrath.

"I said that I'ma die for my motherfucking niggas, most likely I'ma die with my finger on the trigger," my

phone rang interrupting my session. It was my right hand, Rico, calling most likely to update me on business.

"What's good boy?" I answered, inhaling deeply on this new shit called Amazon Kush. I needed this shit to work fast and get my mind on ease quick.

"Yo' nigga, where the fuck you been? We had rounds to make last night!" Rico replied.

"Man, you won't believe this shit," I let out before coughing violently on the Kush. *Damn this some good shit*; I thought before reverting my attention back to my conversation. "Man, I went to that hoe Ashley's house to put a hurting on that pussy and to take a quick four hour nap. Well, I ended up staying over the whole night because the bird brain ass hoe decided to turn my phone off."

As soon as the words left my mouth, I took another long toke of the blunt to ease the anger I felt rising in me. I could hear Rico's ass laughing in the background like I was some nigga on Comedy Central telling jokes and shit

"Ayo' check it, let me go in the house and check on wifey real quick then I'mma be on yo' side in a lil bit," I answered, hanging up the phone not even waiting for that nigga's response.

After ten minutes of taking flight, I quickly jumped out my truck, hit the alarm, and headed for the door. I took a deep breath, put the key in the door, and turned the knob.

"Man Lisa, that bitch ass nigga did not bring his ass home last night. I'm sick of his shit girl for real, for real." I listened to Lala as she sat at the island with her back turned to me venting to her best friend, Lisa. I contemplated if I wanted to speak to her or just walk upstairs and take a shower.

I quickly dismissed that though and spoke up. "What's up bae?" I greeted her calmly hoping like hell she was going to cooperate with a nigga. That thought quickly came to an end when she jumped up off the stool and got in my face.

"What the fuck is wrong with you, James? How dare yo' ass leave this damn house at 7:00 am Thursday morning and not bring your ass into this house until fucking 10:00 am the next day? Where the fuck was yo' ass at for 27 fucking hours?" she yelled, pouting her full lips. Damn that shit along made a nigga's dick jump.

"I was making runs baby, you know I gotta get this money so we can eat." I hit her ass with the I was working late line and hoped like hell she wasn't on that arguing shit early this morning.

Lala looked at me, cocked her head to the side, and laughed. She always did that when shit was about to get out of hand. *WHAM!* Lala bitch smacked my ass like I was some hoe and she was my pimp. Lala's blow had a nigga seeing shooting stars. *This bitch done lost her fucking mind putting her hands on me*: I thought looking at her and clenching tight on my jaw. I grabbed her wrist and bent it behind her back as I pushed her into the wall.

"Lala, I know you're mad, but put your hands on me again like yo' ass crazy and I'mma fuck yo ass up!" I let her ass know, before I pushed her and went upstairs to take a shower. A nigga ain't really have time for that shit right now.

I went into our bedroom and started taking my clothes off. I admired the way Lala designed the room. She always was good with decorating and shit. I saw her medical books on the bed and her scrubs next to them. Thank God she was about to take her ass to school because I did not want to be bothered with her shit today.

Lala knew I loved her ass with all my heart and that no bitch was replacing her. It was just that I was not ready to leave this fast money and bad bitches alone. Growing up, I ain't have shit and couldn't pay a bitch to look my way, but now a nigga was on his throne feeling like a king and I wasn't trying to come down anytime soon. Wrapping the towel around my waist, I entered the bathroom to shower, shit, and shave.

Chapter 2

Lala

I couldn't believe this nigga came in the house a full fucking day later and wanted to put his hands on me. Oh no! I was done with his ass. I'd been with James for eight years now and by the look of things he was not changing. I got up and made my way upstairs.

Passing the hall mirror, I admired myself. I was a real dime piece. Standing at 5'6, my skin was a smooth, caramel color, no blemishes. Bitches paid rent money just to have my long, jet-black, straight hair, and to top it all off, I had a figure to die for.

With my flat stomach, a fat ass, many said I favored Delicious from Flavor of Love some said I looked way better, but all I know was that I was a certified bad bitch and I didn't have to take no nigga's shit. I walked into the bedroom and heard the shower running. Why the fuck is he coming in the house rushing to take a shower?

My women's intuition told me to go through his pockets. I wish I would have ignored it though. I pulled out three Magnums and one of them was an empty wrapper signifying that it was used. The tears instantly poured from my eyes. What the fuck did I do to deserve this shit?

I was nothing but a rider from the day we met. I was 15 and he was 17. I was there when he was broker than the Broke Back Mountains, and uglier than the Ugly Duckling. I could have had any fine hustler, but all of that did not mean shit to me. The person James was who I feel in love with. I was the reason he blew up this big.

I financed his dream of being a major hustler with my afternoon job from Burger King. I was the one who saved my paychecks to help him re-up. I also put my freedom at jeopardy by going to the local mall and stealing him some gear so that he could have the confidence of a baller. How could he do this to me? Did he not know that he could be replaced? Truth was, he knew I wouldn't do it. I was so dangerously in love with James that I couldn't phantom the thought of being without him.

The sound of the bathroom brought me back to this devastating reality. All of that "Baby I'mma change" bullshit he had been giving me instantly angered me.

"What the fuck are these James?" I yelled, throwing the condoms at him as soon as he walked into the room. He just stood there looking down at the condoms like a damn lost puppy. I wanted to slap his ass, but the fear of him slapping my ass back quickly erased that thought out of my mind. I couldn't do it anymore. I walked over to the closet and started pulling my belongings out, tossing them on the bed.

"What the fuck you doing Lala?" he asked getting in my face.

"I'm leaving your trifling ass James, I'm done with you!" I said grabbing my Louis Vuitton luggage out of the closet. I rolled my eyes and was talking shit under my breath while I packed all of my belongings. I felt the tears threaten to spill, but I bit the insides of my cheeks to keep them from falling. I was not going to give this nigga the benefit of seeing me cry over his trifling ass.

"You got life like fucked up," James yelled grabbing me by my neck and pushing me up against the wall. He tightened his grip on my neck a little, just enough to get my attention. "Baby why you always trying to leave me? I'm sorry ma', I know I missed up and I'mma make it right," he whispered in my ear, licking on my neck, while his free hand found its way in my shorts. I gasped when I felt him enter two fingers in me. I instantly let the river flow down his fingers. Damn my body for being so weak to his touch.

"Damn, you so wet, you gon' let daddy hit it?" he groaned in my ear pinching my clit and making it jump.

"Ahhhhh," I moaned as he continued to strum my pain with his fingers, delivering so much pleasure at the same time. I felt like a fool as I let him get to me in the worst way.

He gently lifted me up sitting me on top of the dresser. He pulled my shorts down, keeled before me and had breakfast. The sound of him slurping on my goodies like I was a Popsicle on a scorching hot summer day was turning me on.

"Oh, shit daddy right there!" Right before I could get there, he stopped and looked up at me. His lips looked as if he applied three coats of my Mac lip-gloss as my juices glistened all over his face. "Why did you stop?" I whined trying to push his head back.

"You still leaving?" he asked with a sinister look on his face. He knew he had me, yes he knew I was his. Hell at that point in time I would of sold my heart, lung, and right kidney, just so he could shut up and finish feasting on my kitty.

"No," I answered.

"No what?" he asked sticking his fingers back in to my wet box.

"No, I'm not leaving," I whimpered hoping he would quit playing and bless me with them lips.

"I don't believe you; say it like you mean it," he teased me sucking on my inner thigh.

"James, baby I love you and I'm not going nowhere, I promise." That must have been the key to the door because he dove in headfirst and ate it up. "Yesss gawwwd!" I yelled in pure bliss as he stuck his thick tongue in my furnace, trying to put out the fire that was burning in me. As soon as he felt my love cum down, he sucked every drop as if he have been stranded in the desert and my juices were the answer to his dehydration.

As soon as he was sure that he got every drop of me, he turned me around and entered me with one deep thrust. My pussy walls gripped all nine inches of his thick dick. The impact of the thrust caused me to bump my head on dresser's mirror, but the pain suddenly turned into pleasure when he lifted one of my legs on the dresser and stroked me long and hard. The only sounds that could be heard were the splashes of my wetness, grunts, and moans.

"Damn bae you so wet" he groaned in my ears as he sped up his strokes.

"Oh shit, daddy I'm about to nut!" I yelled out pinching my nipples.

The deeper he plunged the more he pushed me over the edge. I felt like the more he pounded his dick in the hole of my womanhood I was going to float up into the Heavens.

"Nut on daddy's dick, make that shit squirt," he responded pounding away and nailed me as if I was a picture he was trying to hang up on the wall.

Five strokes later, I tightened my pussy muscles and showered him with my sweetness. He stroked me harder and harder signaling that he was close to his peak. I tightened my muscles again this time with enough force to choke his dick. Three strokes later, I felt him release his seeds in me. *Thank God for birth control;* I thought as he stared at me in the mirror.

"I think I put a Jr. in you," he smiled with confidence. I wanted to laugh in his face, but instead I smiled. He was on a first class trip to the crazy house if he thought I was going to have a baby right now. I just started working on my LPN and was currently in school for my RN. Plus I wouldn't dare bring a baby into this world without a ring on my finger or with a nigga that had no ounce of act right in him. Yeah right. He could wait on it.

"Where are you going?" I asked him as he put on a pair of True Religion Jeans.

"I'm going to go meet Rico at the trap and do a few rounds," he replied putting on a pair of white, black, and wolf gray Air Jordan retro nines. He stood up, straightened his shirt, and grabbed his gray and black fitted cap.

"Don't you think you handled enough business last night?' I sassed putting emphasis on the business.

"Lala man, chill out I'm not trying to hear that right now. I'll be back in a few," he told me as he grabbed me around my waist and sucked on my bottom lip. Damn that felt good. The intoxicating scent of his Guilty Gucci cologne was enough to turn on the water faucet between my legs and have it running.

"What time do you have to be at work?" he asked snapping my out of my daze.

"I'm working the 5pm-5am shift today because I have some studying to get done."

"Lala, I told you, you should quit that square ass job and just go to school ma'. I gotchu for real," James said looking at himself in the mirror.

"James, no I am not about to become 100% dependent on you, plus this is a great way to kick start my career as a Head Trauma Nurse," I said. If there was one thing I learned was never to put all of your eggs in one basket. I made sure that I was always able to hold my own.

"Yeah ok, hit me up on your lunch break and I'll come by and take you out," he said kissing me on the forehead. He looked at himself one more time in the mirror and was out the door. *Business my ass;* I thought, watching him get into his car.

I looked over at the clock that was hanging on the wall; damn it was already 1:15pm. I quickly jumped in the shower, handled my business, and jumped out. I decided to moisturize my skin with the Lavender Olay James loved some much. After drying my body and placing lotion all over, I put on a pair of boy shorts by Pink with the matching bra and got down to the little bit of studying I was trying to get done before my shift.

Being a nurse was my passion and I was done putting my dreams on hold for others. After graduation, instead of going to college like I planned, I took a job down at the strip club KOD just to support my man and to help him make it big. I also wanted to stash a little money in my 'being a hustler's wifey' rainy day fund. Now that he was bringing in the dough, it was time for me to pursue my career.

After three hours of studying and writing down important notes; the alarm chirped signaling that it was time to get out the house and head over to Jackson Memorial Hospital. I quickly threw my scrubs on my body, slid my feet into a pair of my pink and purple Air Max, pulled my hair in a high messy bun, applied a light coat of my Mac shimmer, grabbed my books and purse, and was out the door. I got into my apple red Lex, another guilt gift from James, started my ignition, and pulled out of the driveway. R Kelly's voice boomed through my speakers; *"Cuz when a woman's fed up (no matter how you beg, no) it ain't nothing you can do about it."* I listened to the words and wondered was I fed up.

Chapter 3

Stacks

I stepped off the airplane in the Miami International Airport. I was ready to start fresh and according to my pops this was where I had to be. Shit was getting real hot for me back home in Flint, so I had to fall back and start new. I had to come up and this was the place to be and a nigga name James was the one I had to see.

It wasn't like a nigga was hurting; I had a connect, I had money, I just wanted to come in peace and start my operation up. I ain't need no drama coming my way. Well, not yet at least. I had to start all over. Recruit new niggas to put on my team. But, first I had to holla at this nigga James.

He was either going to join my forces, or sink ship. I was a force to be reckoned with back home, so this pressure ain't nothing nice. I only came here with two duffel bags. One with my money and in the other I carried pictures of my girl Donna and sonograms of my twins that I never got meet. Yeah, it was time I left Flint. There were too much bad memories, too many losses; so it was definitely time for a new start.

A honk of a cocaine white BMW X5 snapped me back to reality. Damn, that shit was clean as fuck! The truck came closer to me and pulled into a handicap parking spot that I was standing next to. The passenger rolled down the window and I could see it was my two half-brothers Paco and Pablo. Our father Diego was a big time drug lord in Colombia.

I didn't know the nigga existed until my mother died of breast cancer eight years ago leaving me this letter of how she had an affair with a married man. Apparently, they met when my father made a trip to Atlanta on business and she was there attending Spelman.

They kicked it a few times and she ended up pregnant. When she told him, he finally decided to come clean and confess that he was married. Long story short, she ended up moving back home to Flint so that grandma and grandpa could help her out with me.

What fucked me up was I was this nigga first child. How do you go on in life not being in your first child's life? Although he was never in my life, he made sure to send us money. My mom wrote that she thought it would be good if we got to know each other and we did. At first, I wanted to body that nigga for letting me grow up 17 years without a father, but when he schooled me in this drug game and became my connect, I decided to let him live.

I jumped in the truck and dapped my brothers up. "What's good Paco, Pablo?" I greeted my brothers.

"Cual es hermano a lo grande? *(What is up big brother?)*" Paco replied handing me the blunt that was hanging from his lips.

"What's good Stacks?" Pablo gave me a head nod.

"Nothing, just ready to make shit shake. A nigga ready to get back on his grind," I answered passing the blunt back to Paco.

"I can dig it, but first let's get you set up. I got you a suite at the Mondrian South Beach. I can give you papa's Realtor and she can help you find a nice house."

"Yeah ok," I said looking out the window as we pulled off. A bittersweet feeling came over me. I was happy that I was going to be the KING; however, not having Donna and my twins to share the throne with cut me really deep. If I could trade all this shit in to have them back, I would do it in a heartbeat.

We pulled up to the hotel and it was fly as fuck. I was accustomed to this lavish lifestyle so it didn't really phase me much. "Here you go bro, you're in suite 802.Tthe car that you ordered is already here and is parked in a private garage, lot 13B. If you need anything just call," Pablo said handing me a key card, car keys, and a big brown envelope that I was sure had money in it. I didn't really need the money, but that was our way of telling each other 'I love you'.

"Good looking out bro, link up with y'all later," I said getting out of the car

"Be ready by 9pm, so we can go meet up with this cat James," Pablo responded. I was new to this city and I needed to have some form of backup with me just in case this nigga wanted to be on some funny type shit. Nodding my head, I exited the car and made my way through the crystal glass double doors of the hotel.

"Welcome to Mondrian South Beach!" the sexy ass receptionist flirted, licking her full plump lips.

"Supp ma, I'm looking for the nearest mall, do you think you can help me out?" I smiled at her showing off all thirty-two of the pearliest whites I'd ever seen. She leaned over making sure her double d's spilled out of her vest, giving me a peak-a-boo of the black satin bra that held her girls in place. She was making them sit up high and pretty.

"If you go straight down 32nd and make a right at the light, a quick left, and go straight down the strip you'll fine variety of malls and stores." She looked up at me with those pretty, greens eyes and flashed me a seductive smile. I leaned over the counter making sure my mouth was close to her ear; I blew softly. She gasped. I was sure I heard a thunderstorm; yup I bet I had her raining in her panties.

"Good looking out ma," I whispered in her ear, before I turned around and walked out the crystal doors in search of the garage. Yeah, a nigga still had his shit on pack. Too bad my heart still belonged to a woman I would never get to see, well not in this lifetime at least.

After damn near forty-five minutes of driving around, I was able to locate the strip. I parked my custom made chocolate brown Bentley Continental GT, which I pre-ordered and made sure that it was delivered here before I came. My baby was clean with the cream and peanut butter interior. My ride was worth every penny I dropped on it.

I made my way to the Gucci, Prada, Versace, and Louis stores. Then I entered the mall to get a few tailored suits. I was on my boss man shit. I wasn't like none of these little niggas out here sagging, wearing baggy clothes, and white Tee's and shit. Nah. I was on a whole other level. I was a businessman, not a corner boy.

When I got back to the suit, it was 7:45pm, which meant I had to jump in the shower and get ready for my meeting. I was hoping that everything went well, and that he wanted to team up. I wasn't planning on going at war with this cat, but if that's what he wanted I was going to make sure that nigga felt me in the worst way.

I made my way into the bathroom and got into the shower. I adjusted the water so that it was steaming hot. As soon as the water touched my body, I felt relaxed. So much was going through my head and the feeling of the hot water was enough to relive some of the tension building up in my muscles. I let my mind drift back to the last time conversation Donna and I had…

"Anthony, I am sick and tired of your doggish ways. Here I am six months pregnant with your twins and you still with the bullshit!" Donna yelled, tears falling down here face. I was pissed that the bitch Tasha had a nerve to Instagram a picture of us in bed and tag my fucking girl in it.

My only thoughts at that moment was going to the bitch's house and knocking her head off her fucking shoulders. It killed me when sidepieces forgot their fucking position.

"Baby that picture was old. I swear she's just trying to find a way to fuck up what we got. You can't let these hoes come in between what we have," I reasoned, hoping like hell that she'd believe me. I ain't want her stressing while she had my shorties growing in her womb. I placed my arms around her and brought her to my lap.

"Baby, I promise this will never happen again," I promised, kissing the tears off her beautiful face. Donna was so beautiful. She was half black and half Chinese. She had an erotic type of beauty that you only normally see in high fashion magazines. Every time my eyes fell on her, my heart skipped a beat. I knew from that moment on, she was made for me.

She was everything a man could dream of and more, but the man in me wouldn't allow me to be completely faithful to her. Even though she held two of the most precious possessions a man could ever have inside her, I was still doing her wrong. I held Donna as she cried and promised that I was going to make her my wife. First thing in the morning, I was going to call my jeweler Henry and have him pull some of his best pieces for me.

"Promises are meant to be broken," she quietly whispered. Her sweet angelic voice carried so much pain. My heart cringed at the thought of her leaving me and giving up on our love, I wasn't going to let her go.

"My word is my bond ma."

With that, I laid her down on the bed kissing her with so much passion that all she could do was moan. At that time I wanted to breathe all my love down her throat as our saliva swapped. I wanted her to feel how much I was deeply in love with her. I gently pulled her panties off and French kissed her second sets of lips.

"Mhmmmm baby," she purred. I lunged my tongue deep in her girth using it as a miniature dick. I ate her out like I was on death row and she was my final meal. When I felt her muscle tighten around my tongue, I went to her clit and sucked on it long and hard, gently nibbling on it. I spelled my name over and over and over again in her pussy with nice long strokes until she blessed my mouth with the sweetest nectar ever.

"Turn over," I instructed her. I was ready to get my dick wet and by the way her cum was dripping down her thighs I knew exactly how. I entered her with one, strong, deep thrust and held it there. The pussy was just so tantalizing that I was just moments away from ejaculation and I just got in it. Not wanting to be a minuteman, I quickly gained my composure and slow stroked her.

"Yesssssss daddy! My spot! Oh yesssssssss!!!!" she panted in excitement as the curve in my dick hit her G spot.

"Right where?" I taunted her. Gently rubbing on her nipples.

"R-r-r-right uh mmhm yess oh, yes right there!" I pulled out and dove in deeper. Watching my dick slide in and out of the happiest place earth, I felt my dick swell. If this was heaven then I was done sinning. "Oh, shit daddy I'm about to cuuuuuuum!!" she moaned as her pussy sucked me in deeper causing my knees to get weak.

"Come for daddy," I whispered, stroking her deeper. It was as if my words spoke to her pussy. She made the sexiest love faces and shortly afterwards I felt my dick drowning in her sea. "Oh fuck!" I groaned. Digging deeper and deeper, I was like a leprechaun in search of her pot of gold. My legs got weaker as I returned the favor by flooding her cervix with my nut. If she could get pregnant again, then I'm sure I had just put two more babies in her.

I laid in bed with her until she dosed off. I gently got out of bed to shower and handle business. First thing first I was off to that bitch's house to put my foot up her ass for the stupid shit she pulled, but if I would have known that this would have been me and Donna's last moment together, I would reconsidered and stayed home. Most importantly I would have told her I loved her.

Brrinng! Brrinng! The sound of the hotel's phone brought me back to the hurtful reality. The water turned as cold as my heart did the day the love of my life and children was taken away from me. I got out the shower and answered the phone

"Speak," I snapped a little irritated that my brief moment remembering Donna was interrupted.

"Bro cual tardas tanto yo!! *(Bro, what is taking so long?)*" Paco choked. I could tell he was burning. Looking at the time on the nightstand, I noticed it was 8:30. Damn, I didn't plan on being in the shower so long. I just couldn't help my mind from drifting to the past.

"Damn 15 minutes, voy a estar listo. *(I'll be ready,)*" I replied hanging up the phone to get dress. Even though I didn't grow up with my father, my mother made it her business that I learned her language as well as my father's. I knew how to speak three languages; English, Spanish and Haitian-Creole.

I quickly got dressed; I was never one to arrive anywhere late. I was a firm believer of being there fifteen minutes early just so that I can scope out my surroundings. I checked myself out in the full-length mirror. I looked GQ in my cream Armani suit, and Prada loafers.

The two diamonds I wore in each ear shined brighter than the Miami's sun itself. I put on my Hublot Classic Fusion Haute Joaillere watch, sprayed some Prada cologne on me, and I was good to go. A nigga walked out the room looking like a million dollars; well my watch alone was worth that much. So I wasn't new to this shit. I said a quick prayer and got in the car with my brothers.

Chapter 4

James

I sat at The Morton's Steakhouse waiting for this nigga Stacks who was looking to do business with me. I told this nigga 9:00pm and it was now 9 fucking 30! I was about to get up and grab Ashley and go, but then I spotted niggas in suits being escorted to our table by the host. Who the fuck they thought they were? Men in fucking Black or some shit. This shit was comical to me already.

"Sorry we're late, I just flew in town," the nigga who I was assuming to be Stacks spoke.

I reached over and gave him a pound and the ice he wore on his wrist blinded the fuck out of me. That nigga looked and smelled like money, so I decided to stay and chop it up to see what he was all about.

"Nah, it's straight," I replied sizing him up, trying to add up how much money his attire cost.

"Can I get you guys some drinks?" the white preppy waitress asked with a note pad in her hand, snapping me out my thoughts.

"Get us a few bottles of Patron," I spoke, looking over at Ashley who was practically eye-fucking Stacks. I wanted to slap this hoe in the mouth for looking so fucking thirsty. The only reason I brought her ass because wifey ended up picking up an extra shift and I assumed Stacks was bringing his girl so I didn't want to come alone looking like a fool. I instantly regretted my decision bringing this dehydrated looking bitch with me. Clearing my throat I spoke up. "So Stacks, what brings you to the MIA?" I asked wanting to know why the fuck this nigga decided to come in my town.

"Well, shit back in Flint was getting dry and I needed to relocate to make big moves," he answered taking a sip of the water that the waiter placed on the table all the while looking me directly in the eyes.

"Ok, so what's your proposition?" I said getting right to it. There was no need for beating around the bush.

"I want you to work for me," he simply replied with a cocky ass demeanor as if it was that easy. Did he not know who the fuck he was talking to?

"Work for you?" I asked making sure I heard this fool correctly. I furrowed my eyebrows matching his intense gazed. This nigga was on some Ashton Kutcher punk shit. There was an awkward silence and I could tell somewhere in some hospital a gay baby was being born.

"I was looking to recruit niggas, set up shops, and supply. I want you on my team as one of my lieutenants. You'll run your same areas with your same guys, but I'd be the one supplying you," he answered, declining the cup of Patron the waitress offered him. I took a sip of my drink and allowed the strong liquor to run down my throat.

"What if I'm not trying to step down and work for you?" I said pouring another drink.

"Whether you're on my team or not I'm still going to move my weight. I just thought I'd come to you with a proposition instead of coming in and taking over," he smirked.

I downed the rest of my drink to calm the anger that I felt brewing in my system. The nerve of this nigga to come on my territory and offer me a job like I was some bum ass nigga. He should be the one asking me for a job. I took a look at the two Spanish cats that were sitting by his side and wondered who the fuck they were supposed to be. I tried to read their facial expression, but I got nothing.

"Well, I am not about to lay down and let nobody take what I worked so hard for!" I raised my voice a little because the thought of him trying to demote a nigga had me feeling some type of way. Miami was my city!

"Understandable, well I guess I will be running my operation without you then," he had the nerve to say, glancing over at Ashley and throwing her ass one of those flirtatious winks.

"Over my dead body!" I spat, standing up ready to body this nigga right here, not giving the fuck that I was outnumbered.

"Eso se puede arreglar, *(that can be arranged)*" One of his Chiquita Taco Bell looking niggas spoke, mean mugging me.

"Speak English, motherfucker! In case yo' ass ain't get the memo, you're in America!" I grilled his ass matching his mug.

"You sure you want to do this because once I walk out them doors the offer leaves with me?" Stacks spoke calmly, a little too calm for me.

"Nah, I'm good. I can run things in my city, MY city. So go on to the next nigga's turf with all that." I wasn't giving up my throne for no fucking body; I was the king of Miami!

Stacks laughed as if I was Kevin Hart or some shit. I didn't find shit funny. "Well, like I said with or without you, I will start my operation," he said as he stood up and straightened his jacket "It was nice meeting you," he said giving Ashley's hand a kiss. The bitch actually had the nerve to be blushing. "See you around," he spoke to me, walking out, and taking his two G-I Joe dolls with him. I threw three hundred dollar bills on the table and stood to leave.

"Wow that was like some shit straight out of one of those gangster's movies," Ashley rabbit ass spoke as the Valet brought the car around.

WHAM! I slapped the shit out of her ass the moment we got in the car. "How the fuck you gon' embarrass me like that?" I yelled punching her ass in the nose. Blood shot out of her nose staining the interior in my car pissing me off even more. "Get the fuck out of my car hoe!" I was ready to drag her ass out.

"How am I supposed to get home?" she cried, cradling her nose that I was sure I broke.

"You should have thought about that shit before you was smiling all in the next nigga's face, now bitch get the fuck out!" I yanked the passenger's door open, pulling her out by the long ass weave I was sure she bought with my money.

"Please James, don't do this to me! I'm sorry!!" she cried, looking pathetic. I almost felt bad for the bitch. I reached in my pocket and threw her five-twenties.

"You got one fucking hour to bring your ass home, get there any later and I swear I'mma fuck you up!" I yelled as I got in my car and pulled off.

***

I pulled into Ashley's driveway and made my way in the house. The smell of garbage instantly insulted my nostrils. *Nasty ass rat*; I thought as I looked around at this filthy ass place. I put her in a three-bedroom condo and financed her ass. All she had to do was be my on call hoe.

What fuck did she do in her spare time that she couldn't keep her fucking house clean? There were dirty dishes in the sink, hair weave on the counter, and three garbage bags filled with trash. Lala would have never allowed our home to look this disgusting and that was why she was wifey and Ashley was just a thot.

The headlights of a car caught my attention. I walked to the window to see who the fuck was pulling up. I swear if this bitch had a nigga coming the house I paid for I was deading him and her hoe ass. I watched as Ashley got out of a cab, paid the driver, and made her way to the front door. Her nose was done bleeding, but it was swollen. I should fuck her dumbass up some more.

"Take yo ass in the bathroom and get yourself cleaned up! And clean this fucking house!" I barked at her as soon as she closed the front door. "I'm hungry too." I left her ass downstairs to her follow my orders. I stripped down to my boxers then got in bed. I scrolled through my phone and saw a text notification from wifey.

Wifey: *I miss you ☐ wish I was in bed with you.*

Me: miss you too baby, what time are you getting off?

Wifey: *6am, and you better be in bed waiting on me! I'm not playing with your ass either James!!!*

Me: *lol I gotchu baby, I'm about to get some sleep, love you bae.*

Wifey: *ok. Love you too bye baby.* I quickly read the message and set my alarm for 4am and made myself comfortable.

Ashley walked in the room in a robe, sitting my food on the nightstand. *At least she know how to cook;* I thought as I inhaled the chicken and shrimp Alfredo she prepared me. I immediately scarfed the food down and gulped down the cherry Kool-Aid all in five minutes. A nigga was famished.

As soon as I finished, I put the plate in the sink and noticed the kitchen was finally cleaned. Good thing I ain't have to put my foot in her ass because all I wanted to do was lay down and get some sleep before going home to my girl. On my way back in the room, I saw her in the bathroom nursing her nose. She looked at me to see if I would apologize or some shit.

That bitch had me fucked up, she got what she deserved. Maybe if her nose was disfigured she'd lose her confidence and stop trying to act brand new around niggas. As far as I was concerned, she was my bitch until I was done playing with her ass and ready to fully commit to Lala.

Chapter 5

Ashley

As soon as James' alarm went off, he got up, got dressed, and went home to his bitch. I don't know why he always went home to that slut. I had everything he needed right. He always fed me that 'oh she's loyal, I love her, we're gonna get married one day' bullshit, but I was just as loyal as she was.

In fact, she wasn't even half the woman that I was. She couldn't even give James a baby. He was always talking about how bad he wanted a child, but every time we had sex he'd strap up. Maybe if I got pregnant with his first child he'd leave her alone and stay with me.

I know you're wondering why I would want to be with a man who just probably broke my nose. Truth was, I love him so much. He was not always this jerk and I absolutely adored him. The only problem was, Lala's bourgeois ass! I had to think of a master plan quick. I needed my man home with me at night.

Looking in the mirror, I noticed my nose was really swollen. I hated when he got in his feelings and started acting abusive and shit. I gently held a cold towel on it hoping it would help a little. I had things to do. It was jumping off tonight at KOD for Kendrick Lamar's birthday bash and I wasn't missing it for shit.

I hurriedly got dressed and was out the door to meet up with my best bitch Loye.

***

"Yessssss bitch, you better werk!" Loye smacked his lips and flipped his long, blonde wig as he waited for me to come sit in his chair.

"Sup hoe." I sat down crossing my legs.

"Oooh, baby what the fuck happened to your nose? Look like Starkiesha got a hold of your ass," he laughed.

"Bitch, ain't shit funny, but James hit me," I said regretting telling his extra dramatic ass that.

"He did what!!? Oh, no bitch, you ain't fuck his ass up?" his ass yelled out being so extra.

"Yes, I showed that nigga not to fuck with me!" I lied. I was not about to let Loye know I got beat on a regular. He'd been my best friend since we were five and what he thought of me mattered.

"So, what am I doing to your hair miss?" he said grabbing the scissors to cut the tracks out my hair.

"You see how Beyoncé's bob was in 'Drunk In Love'? That's what I want, but instead of blond I want red." I was going to be that baddest bitch in KOD tonight.

"Yessssssss bitch, when I'm done with you, Beyoncé is going to be calling me personally." He smacked his lips and got to work. We chatted about how turnt up we was going to be tonight while he worked his magic on me.

"Viola!!!" Loye said, turning me around so that I could view my hair in the full-length mirror. This bitch did the damn thing in my hair. I was living for my new do and at that moment, my confidence level shot through the roof. You couldn't tell me shit; I was feeling myself!

"Yes bitch, you did you damn thing." I hugged him, still amazed on how I was killing this do. I couldn't wait to get home and get dressed. The turn up was about to be too real! "Please be ready a 9pm." I gave Loye a serious look. He was known to have a bitch waiting years for his ass to get dress.

"Don't do me fish, just be outside," he rolled his eyes and popped his gum, propping his hand on his hips. He was a true diva for real.

As soon as I got home, I saw James sitting on my couch smoking a blunt. A part of me was scared, but the other part of me was happy as fuck.

"Where the fuck you been?" he calmly asked. I was grateful that the weed had his ass on chill mode. I wasn't trying to fight and have him fuck around and pull one of my tracks out.

"Just went and got my hair done. You like it?" I twirled around giving him a view, putting a little bounce in my ass so it could jiggle.

"Come suck this dick," he said, taking another pull of his blunt. Like the good bitch I was, I crawled over to my man to blow his mind. Pulling his dick out, I licked the head and sucked on it using all my jaw muscles. I felt his dick twitch, so I gathered all the saliva in my mouth and spit it all on the dick, making it real nasty.

I took him deep in my mouth; slurping and sucking him like a 7-11 Slurpee. I let his dick pop out of my mouth and used it to slap me across the face. I relaxed my throat then took him deep in my mouth.

"Damn ma," he groaned, closing his eyes. I went down deeper again, this time fitting his whole dick and his balls in my mouth. I squeezed my throat muscles around his dick and held it there. "Oh shit, bae damn! Like that?" he moaned and I gently pulled my panties off and slid down on his dick.

"Mmmhmm." He felt so damn good. I rocked my hips making sure to make it real tight for him. I was determined to get pregnant; I was ovulating so all I needed was for him to slip up and nut in me. I rocked back and forth faster and faster. He was so close to nutting and the thought of me being his main lady motivated me more. I spread my legs wide, putting them on both over the arms of the chair so that I was straddling him in a spilt position. I used my arms to balance myself as I twerked on his dick.

"Oh, shit girl slow down," he said above a whisper as I felt his dick twitch in me. Bingo! He was almost there, so I sped it up more and bounced my ass up and down on the dick with no mercy. A few strokes later he pushed me off his dick and nutted on the floor. That shit made me so mad, but I couldn't let it show on my face.

"That was some good shit," he said, smacking me on the ass while walking to the bathroom to clean himself off. *Damn! I have to get him one way or another I was determined to have his baby;* I thought as I then came up with my bright idea. I walked over to the cabinet that held the condoms. I grabbed a small thumbtack and poked small holes at the tip of the rubber. Once I was done, I went into the bathroom for round two. Yes, I was going to have his baby voluntarily or involuntarily; the choice was his.

After our two-hour fuck fest, he left and went home. I was feeling real good inside, the thought of me carrying James' baby had a Kool-Aid smile plastered on my face.

He left me no choice, a woman had to do what a woman had to do. I decided to cook something to eat and watch a few movies until it was time to go out.

Once it hit 8pm, I got up to shower. I douched my pussy with the Summer's Eve Douche. I planned on popping this coochie all night and I ain't want no foul order coming from between my legs. After I made sure every crevice of my body was cleaned, I jumped out the shower to brush, floss, and gargle.

I hated a bitch with bad breath, so I refused to be one of them. I walked over to my closet to find something that would drop jaws to the floor as soon as I walked through the doors. After what seemed like forever, I decided to wear my short black Michael Kors tight 'fuck me' dress with the drop neckline. I oiled up my body and slipped on my dress, no bra no panties. I put on my gold MK heels, sprayed my body with some Japanese Blossom from Bath and Body works, grabbed my matching gold clutch, and was out the door.

Twenty minutes later, I pulled up in front of Loye's apartment. It was 9:30 so his ass better be ready or I was leaving him. I laid on the horn, honking it unmercifully. I saw a few of his neighbor's peek their heads through the window, trying to figure out what was all the commotion. I guess I was disturbing their peace, as if I gave a fuck.

Loye strutted his, or shall I saw her ass down the driveway and into my car. The diva was dressed in drag tonight and he was looking fierce honey. I peeped him out in his orange and gold Vera Wang romper, on his perfectly pedicured feet was a pair of gold Prada wedges, his make-up was flawless and that long straight honey blond wig had him looking like a natural born woman.

"Yessssssss bitch, you better werk," I said as he got in the car.

"You see me boo?" he replied, applying more Mac gloss to his already glossy plum lips. The guys at KOD was in for a rude awaking when they realized that 'she' was actually a 'he'.

We pulled up in front of the club where I went through valet to have my car parked. We made our way to the front of the line. Teddy was the bouncer and one of Loye's undercover playmates. There was no way in hell that we were standing in line tonight.

As soon as Teddy noticed us, he gave us a wink, which I knew was mainly for Loye and he let us in.

'Bounce bounce bounce bounce bounce bounce bounce bounce bounce bounce bounce bounce bounce bounce bounce bounce, bounce that ass up and down' Alyric's *'Bounce dhatt ass'* boomed through the speakers and nothing but asses was bouncing.

I made my way to the dance floor and decided to bounce my ass too. My bitch Loye decided to join me on the floor and together we fucked shit up. Some of the ballers took their attention away from the strippers and was making it rain on us. Feeling myself, I decided to drop my ass low popping my coochie giving nothing but pussy shots.

I heard a few of the strippers suck their teeth; hell they should have had their notepad out taking notes. The niggas was making it storm on my ass. Hurricane Ashley came through and straight took food out of all these stripper hoes' mouth. I gladly bent over showing all my ass as I collected my coins. Shit! I hope they ain't think I was leaving this money on the floor for them.

"Damn bitch, the whole world and their mamas was looking all in your goodie box," Loye said, taking a sip of his Rum and Coke. "Let James would have been in here and he would have knocked yo ass back into last week," he laughed.

"James don't run shit," I lied knowing damn well he'd break my jaw if he knew I was in here with no draws on.

"You need to drop that no good ass nigga anyways. He expects you to be at his beck and call when he runs home to Lala every night." He sucked his teeth, taking another sip of his drink.

"What about you? You fucking with three married men," I snapped, feeling myself getting mad.

"I surely do, but when they run back home to their wife, I'm free to do me," he said, making me feel like shit.

"Yeah whatever, are we going to talk about my love life or have fun?" I was hoping to change the subject.

"Turn up then!" And that's exactly what we did.

After the club, we decided to go to IHOP to grab some breakfast. As soon as we got inside, I was instantly enraged. Smoke must have been coming out my ears because Loye was looking at me trying to figure out why my mood had suddenly changed.

I was livid, James was booed up with this bitch feeding her pancakes and shit like he just wasn't beating this pussy up a few hours ago. I know James ain't my man, but the thought of him being with anyone else besides me had me outraged. Deciding to have some fun, I slipped the hostess a 50-dollar bill to sit us right next to them

"I am so ready for exams to be over Bae, this semester is kicking my ass," I overheard Lala's bitch ass say to James while eating a fork filled with eggs.

"Bae, I told you I gotchu. You don't need to be stressing. All you have to worry about is having my baby," he replied back to her. I was on ten. I got something for that ass though. The waitress came over and asked us for our drinks we ordered and I decided to put my plan into motion.

"Loye, I can't believe this nigga ain't call me all day. I'm about to call his ass right now to see what's up," I said loud enough so that James could hear my voice. I smirked when I saw how James almost choked on his steak when he looked up and confirmed that it was I, in the flesh, sitting right next to him and 'wifey'.

"Girl call him and ask him to come over here with a friend, shit I'm still trying to turn up," Loye said, smiling as he caught on to what I was doing. I picked up my phone to dial James' number and out the corner of my eyes, I saw him trying to discreetly put his phone on silent.

He wasn't quick enough because his phone started to ring. I popped my gum and decided to put my phone on speaker just so his bitch could know that it was me all in her nigga's call log. James was trying to keep his cool, but in his draws I know he shitted bricks. The icing on the cake was when the lady on his voice mail loud and clear informed me that my call was forwarded to an automated voice message system, read off his number, and asked me to leave a message after the tone.

I looked his bitch right in the eye and said, "Bae call me back when you get this message. Matter fact come over when you down playing house with your bitch." I hung up the phone, threw a twenty-dollar bill on the table, and got up. Lala was still looking at me like she wanted to do something, so I decided to provoke her ass. "Hoe I got yo boyfriend, hoe I can take yo man. I can put it on him just like he want it. Like, I got yo man," I rapped the lyrics to Khia' song letting the hoe know what was up and left. He ain't getting pussy tonight! I laughed, putting an extra bounce in my ass.

***

"You know James going to fuck you up right?" Loye said, taking off his heels when we got inside my condo.

"Yeah I know, but at least he won't be digging in that hoe's guts tonight." I smiled to myself, happy because I knew I created some type of drama between them. With any luck, she would do the smart thing and leave his ass all to me.

"I know that's right," Loye said, bringing me back to realty. We gave each other a high five as we laughed. I knew James would be over here as soon as he got a chance to put his foot up my ass and I ain't care. If I played my cards right, I wouldn't have to worry about that bitch no more. I got up and made us some breakfast since we didn't get to eat breakfast at IHOP.

My phone vibrated signaling that I had a text.

James: *you play so much, I'ma fuck you up fr!*

I showed Loye the text and we fell out laughing, but deep down inside I was scared as fuck!

Chapter 6

Lala

"Let me go, James! I'm going to spend the night over Lisa's house. I can't stand to be around yo' ass no more I swear!" I yelled in his face trying to break free. This nigga had me all types of fucked up if he thought I was going for this shit.

"Lala man just chill and hear me out man for real. I ain't trying to hear you leaving and shit." He tried to restrain me, but all that did was pissed me off more. He lucky we was in the bedroom because if I had a knife in my possession I would have been cut his dirty dick off and handed it right to him.

"James, let me go clear my head please! Just let me go," I cried, trying to break free. I was so sick and tired of this nigga's shit. When would he learn to appreciate the good woman that I was? How many years of this bullshit did I have to put up with until he finally woke the fuck up and smelled the damn Folgers?

He was never going to grow the fuck up and that was something that I had to choose if I wanted to deal with or not. I was everything a man could ask for, but this nigga was too damn dumb to realize it. He wanted to fuck with childish ass hoes.

Instead of her stepping up to me like a woman, she wanted to play high school games. Like, who still did shit like that? She was lucky I ain't snatch that raggedy ass bob she had in her head off. Cheap ass bitch wasn't on my level; she was still wearing shit that came out three years ago. Her pussy must have not been so good if she couldn't get James to upgrade her ass.

His phone started to ring, distracting him. As soon as he loosened his grip on me to reach for it, I hauled ass. I got in my car and speed off before he could catch up to me. I felt my phone ringing and I tried to dig in my purse to pick it up.

BOOM!!

Shit; I thought as I crashed into the back of an all-black Maserati. *Fuck man, I'm not on this shit tonight.* I put my car in park and got out.

As soon as I headed towards the driver of the car I hit, I was at lost for words. This man was so damn fine. Good lawd!

"I-I-I'm sorry," I stuttered on my words. I was knocked off my square a little. I wasn't expecting to see this fine ass man standing here looking so damn sexy! The only man that was able to have my juices flowing off of looks alone was James and this dude here had James beat! "I'll write down my insurance info and I'm sure they'll cover the damages." I looked into his hazel eyes. He licked his lips.

"Nah, Ma' you good. It was an accident right?" he smiled showing off his deep dimples.

"Yes, but it was my fault, so you should let me fix it," I said trying to delete all the naughty thoughts I had dancing around in my head.

"It's ok. I can get it fixed; it's no big deal. Why were you such in a rush anyways?" He leaned his tall frame against the hood of my car and pulled a blunt from behind his ear.

"Long story," I answered, taking in his muscular frame. He looked so scrumptious in his gym shorts and wife beater.

"I got time. Want to grab a cup of coffee?" He smiled making me melt for the third time since we met.

"Uh umm," I stammered, lost on how to reply to his offer.

"I won't bite. This will make up for you crashing into my car. Follow me," he said, walking off like he just knew for sure that I was going to follow him. He got in his car and waited for me to get in mine. It felt so wrong, but something in me wanted to be around him a little longer. Once he saw that I was in my car, he pulled off and my Curious George ass followed him.

Once we pulled up in front of the small mom and pop's coffee shop on 73rd street. He put money in his meter; in the one I was parked at, and then came over to open my door for me. When we made it inside the coffee shop, we ordered our drinks and sat down in the far back corner next to an old couple making out like they were in high school.

"So are you going to tell me why you were speeding?" He looked at me, taking a sip of his Mocha.

"I don't even know your name." I took a bite of my cheese Danish, trying to change the subject a little.

"I'm sorry, where are my manners? I'm Anthony, but I go by Stacks You?" He smiled, showing me those deep dimples again.

"Lala," I replied.

"Lala? That's pretty. It fits you."

I instantly felt my cheeks getting rosy red. For some reason, I loved the way he said my name.

"So Stacks, I haven't seen you around, where you from?" I asked taking a look at my vibrating phone, then putting it back in my bag.

"I'm from Flint, I just moved down here." He kept it short, like it was something he was hiding.

"What made you want to move to Miami?" I probed wanting to know more.

"Business purposes. Enough about me, tell me about you," he said licking those lips again. He was hypnotizing me with the way his sexy ass was looking at me.

"What do you want to know?" I said, crossing my legs. I was afraid if I didn't plug this drain I would flood the streets with the wetness that sat in the seat of my crotch.

"Everything," he shrugged.

"Well I'm 23, I was born and raised in the county of Dade. I'm currently a LPN at Jackson Memorial Hospital and I'm in school trying to get my degree to become a registered nurse. I want to be a Trauma Nurse, to be exact," I replied with confidence. I was a black woman who had her shit together and I was proud of my accomplishments and myself.

"Sounds good. So tell me this Ms. Lala do you have a Mr. Lala?" he smoothly asked. I looked down at my ring finger and showed him that there wasn't any 'Mr.' in my life.

"No, but I do have a boyfriend," I said remembering the hurtful truth. Although my man was no good, this was wrong on so many levels. I had no business being out here at 6am with a man that wasn't James. "It was nice meeting you Stacks, but I have to get going." I suddenly felt ashamed.

"The pleasure was all mines, but let me have your number. I just want to make sure you got home safely."

I hesitated at first, but shrugged it off. I put my number in his phone, got in my car, and headed to Lisa's house.

I parked my car and made my way inside using my key. I walked to Lisa's room and saw her sleeping with *"Think Like A Man"* on TV, but watching her instead of her watching it. I took off my shoes, stripped down to my boy shorts, and bra and climbed in bed with her.

Lisa has been my best friend since we was in our mother's wombs. Both of our mother's planned to get pregnant by dope boys in high school and here we were today. Born on the same day, month, year only I was older by five hours. Since I was my mother's only child, she was the closet thing I had to a sister. I cherished our friendship and I would seriously kill for her.

"Why are you in my bed big head?" she asked, sitting up in her bed. Lisa was a very light sleeper; she could hear a feather drop on the ground in her sleep. No words had to be spoken as the tears started to fall as I cried in her arms. This was nothing new to her; this was our routine. I just thanked God that I had a good friend like her. She gently rocked me back and forth a listened as I vent, until sleep took over my body.

***

"Who is Stacks?" Lisa asked as soon as my eyes opened up.

"Stop being so damn nosey!" I said, snatching my phone from her. I looked at the message that read: *Hey beautiful just checking on you to see if you made it home without wrecking any more cars. LOL. I really enjoyed our short time together tho. So when your man ain't around hmu and let me know that you're ok. Stacks.*

Reading that text had me feeling like the finest boy in the school just asked me to prom. I could not hold back the smile that threatened to appear on my face.

I made it home safely thanks for asking. Good morning btw. I replied to his text and then went through the other bullshit messages that I got from James.

"So, who is he?" Lisa asked trying clock my T's.

"Some guy I met coming over here. I crashed into his car and we had coffee," I nonchalantly said, getting up to brush my teeth.

"So, does this mean no more James?" she asked, standing next to me as she grabbed her toothbrush.

"I don't know," I told her as we brushed our teeth in silence.

"Well, when will you know, Lala? I'm sick and tired of that boy breaking your heart. He is a rotten apple and there is no fixing that." I sat there and let the tears pour down my face. I knew she was right; I just didn't want to accept it.

"So, what are we doing today?" Lisa asked, sitting next to me at the table and then poured her a bowl of cereal.

"I wanted to get my hair done, do a little shopping, and maybe go out tonight," I answered, ignoring another one of James' calls.

"Ok. Where you trying to go tonight?" she asked with a mouth full of Coco Puffs.

"What about club Mansion?" I suggested.

"I'm down," she replied swigging her spoon in the air. We shared a laugh until Monica interrupted us; *I got loooooooooooove all over me, baby you touch every part in me.* My phone rang for the 25th time, letting me know James was still trying to get some conversation out of me. I got up from the table and answered the phone.

"What the fuck do you want James?!!"

"Lala, baby when you coming home?" he asked sounding so pathetic.

"I need some more time to think, James, I think we need some time apart." I tried to sound confident in my decision, but in reality I just wanted to run home into his arms.

"Lala, that shit you spitting don't even make sense. Come home ma', please?" he begged.

"Just give me some more time," I said before hanging up. I had to end that call. I was a sucker for James and he would have been able to convince me into coming back home.

***

We made our way through Aventura mall maxing out James' black card. I had my own money, but since he put a hurting on my heart I decided to put one in his pockets with some retail therapy. After we maxed out his card, we decided to go to Stars nails and get our hair and nails done.

As soon as I sat down in the seat to get my pedicure, I spotted the tramp from IHOP. I looked her up and down, yeah she was bad, but I was badder hands down. All she needed was an upgrade in her style and she could possibly compete with me. At least this hoe James decided to cheat on me with didn't look busted down like the others. I sat in the chair, winked at her then pulled out my phone to text James.

Me: *I'm sitting right here next to your bitch. I should fuck her up for that little stunt she pulled.*

Don't get it wrong, I was every bit of classy; however, if a female fucks with a dude knowing he has a chick at home, she deserved to get that ass whooped.

James: *Bae just chill and come home, fuck that hoe.*

Me: *I'll come home when I'm ready.*

I turned my phone off and put it back in my bag. I was not going to let James or his bitches stress me out.

After we were done getting dolled up, Lisa and I decided to head down to Chili's to get something to eat. We were hungry after shopping and getting pretty all day.

"Welcome to Chili's," the geeky looking hostess greeted us with a smile that showed of his braces. "Is it just you two?" He still had that goofy ass smile stuck on his face.

"Yes it is," I said.

"Ok, right this way ladies." He sat us at our table, took our orders for our drinks, and left.

"Girl, you won't believe who I saw in Stars Nails," I said to Lisa as I scrolled down my Facebook page.

"Who??" Lisa asked with her nosey ass. Ever since I'd been friends with her, she'd always been nosey. If you had the tea she would come running to you with her cup and sugar.

"The IHOP hoe," I laughed at the little nickname I gave her.

"No, you didn't. Why you ain't come tell me?" One thing about Lisa was she was about that life. You couldn't tell her nothing without her wanting to pop off.

"Girl I wasn't trying to go to jail over a hoe that ain't worth it. Fuck him and fuck her," I said trying to convince myself that it was really fuck him.

"And in that order!" she co-signed impersonating Mama Dee

. "Are you ladies ready to order?" the waiter asked as he sat our drinks in front of us.

"Yes, I'll have the half rack baby back ribs with loaded mashed potatoes, and broccoli," I responded, handing him my menu

"I will also have what she's having," Lisa said taking a sip of her Coke.

"Lisa, do you think it'll be ok if I crashed at your house for a few days?" I asked with a mouth full of ribs.

"Girl, what type of question is that? Mi casa is a su casa." We bust out laughing at her failed attempt to say the phrase in Spanish. For the remainder of lunch, we ate in silence. The food was too good and both of us were too hungry to focus on anything else but our plates. After we were done with lunch, we went back to the house to pop some popcorn and watch movies.

"What we watching?" Lisa came in the living room with an oversized bowl of popcorn and two bottles of water.

"Paid In full," we both said together.

I didn't even know why she asked. Every time we had a movie night, we watched this movie first. This was like our signature movie, besides Mekhi Phifer being so damn fine; the snake in their circle reminded us of the snake Katrina that use to be in ours.

Around 9pm, we decided to get up and get ready for the club. I laid out my under garments and went to take a bubble bath. I filled the tub with warm water. I poured some of my Victoria's Secret Angel bubble bath gel into the water and got in.

The water felt so good against my skin and for the first time in forever I felt relaxed. I still missed James and a part of me wanted to text him to see if he was ok. I knew that I was going back, but I had to show him how it felt to not have me, then maybe he'd get a dose of act right. After 30 minutes of soaking my body, I got up, lathered my loofah, and soaped my body from head to toe. I turned on the shower to rinse my body off then I got out the tub.

"Can you put some damn clothes on?" I said to Lisa. She was standing in front of the mirror naked while applying her makeup.

"Hoe please you know you like this ass," she said making it bounce up and down. Even though we both use to work at KOD, she still decided to work there. I often tried to convince her to go back to school, but hey she loved the life of being a stripper.

After moisturizing my body with my lavender Olay, I put on my nude laced thong, and wiggled my fat ass into my Donna Karan soft pink bandage dress. The whole left sleeved and back was cut out showing the dimples I had in my back. My ass was too much for the dress to hold as the material of the dress held onto my curves for dear life.

I didn't need to wear a bra because my pretty perky D-cups sat up nice in the dress. I put on my jeweled clear and soft pink Jimmy Choo heels and accessorized my dress with my diamond-studded choker with the matching bracelet. I put my massive diamond studs in my ears and I was set. My face was flawlessly beautiful, so I only applied just a touch of make-up.

Making sure my lips looked extra juicy, I applied an extra coat of my Mac Nude shimmer gloss. Passing the hallway mirror, I stopped to admire myself. I was looking BAD! Too bad James couldn't see the good he had right in front of his eyes. I wasn't just a pretty face with an hourglass figure to die for; I was legit wifey material, the type of chick you brought home to moms. The lady in the bed and the freak in the sheets type chick.

I went down stairs and saw Lisa looking through her purse making sure she had everything. She was known to leave her ID or some other important shit always having us to turn back around. She looked real good in her high waist shorts, white crop top, mustard colored blazer, and some mustard colored red bottoms. We took a few pictures for IG and were on our way.

Lisa decided to pull out the all back everything Beamer. We got in, dropped the top, and were on our way like Ice Burg. Who was fucking with us tonight? Nobody. Call it arrogance, but I called it confidence!!

***

The line for club Mansion was wrapped around the building. There was no way in hell that we were going to just stand out here and wait in line though. We walked to the front of the line and just like that we were granted entrance. A few birdbrain bitches sucked their teeth and whined, but who gave a fuck. Being the wifey of James, the "King of Miami", and having a face and body like ours came with a lot of perks.

As soon as we walked in, it was as if the DJ knew we was coming to shut shit down because he had *Bad Bitches* by Tyga blasting through the club's speakers. Me and my best bitch got on the dance floor and showed the fuck out. Yes, we were two of the baddest bitches in here indeed.

After dancing to five songs back to back, we decided to take our seat in our VIP section. There were a few bottles of Remy Martin VSOP, in a big bucket of ice waiting for us. We got our drink on and were ready to get real live. Tonight not James or his bitches was going to get the best of me. I was ready to unwind and have fun. I was young, so why not? Lisa was on the dance floor dry fucking some dude so I decided to join her. TURN DOWN FOR WHAT?

Chapter 7

Stacks

I was out celebrating with my new team. I wasn't big on partying, but my day one nigga Bear came down to help me out with my business. Pops just set me up real nice and I had close to 3,300 Kilos of the good shit stashed away at my spot. Nobody knew that I had that much weight, not even my brothers. I learned in the game you couldn't trust anyone. Snakes came in all shapes and sizes.

If everything went as planned, I would be bringing in 330 million dollars. I was so ready to take on the streets of Miami. I had my crew, my traps, and an army of niggas who was ready to put in work. James was a fool to pass up the opportunity to make this paper with me. I had no choice but to permanently put his connect to rest. He was the king? Nah fuck that, I'm the new King!

"Damn Stacks look at them two bad bitches on the dance floor," Bear said snapping me out of my money train of thoughts. I took a look to where he was pointing and there was that chick Lala. She was a real bad one. When she crashed into the back of my car, I was pissed, but as soon as my eyes fell on her my heart skipped a beat.

That shit was crazy because after I lost Donna no woman had that effect on me. A part of me wanted to get to know her more. She just seemed so different than these thirsty hoes I've encountered so far.

I made my way to the dance floor. The DJ was spinning *How Many Drinks* by Miguel. I grabbed her by the waist, pulled her close to me, and started singing in her ear.

"Frustration, watching you dance. Invitation, to get in them pants. Come closer baby, so I can touch. One question, am I moving too fast? Cause I ain't leaving alone, feel like I could be honest babe we both know that we're grown that's why I want to know, how many drinks would it take you to leave with me?" I felt her grind her hips on my dick so I held onto her firmly so she could feel

the anaconda come alive. I licked her ears and sung the rest of the song to her while she got her grind on. When the song ended, she turned around and looked at me.

"I ain't know you could sing," she said, but I knew what she really wanted to say was 'bend me over and fuck me right here on the spot'.

"There's a lot of things you don't know about me ma," I said kissing her on the hand and walking away. I could feel her eyes burning a hole in my back. I smiled knowing it was only a matter of time before she would come looking for me.

"Damn bra, that's you?" Bear asked as soon as I sat back down.

"No, but if she play her cards right she could be," I laughed, taking a sip of my drink. There was something about Lala that I couldn't shake. She was beautiful, smart; she had her self together, and that body! Man, I ain't seen a body like that in years. Donna had a nice body, but Lala's body was on a whole other level. I was usually able to control my Jr., but the way that ass was rubbing on me Jr. said fuck that and decided to stand up.

I sat and watched her and her and her home girl dance. I was mesmerized by her. She had me feeling like I felt every time I laid my eyes on Donna. It'd been a year since her and my twins died and I never fully got over her. I fucked a few bitches to get my rocks off, but nothing serious as dating, but laying my eyes on Lala changed that. It was beyond sex. I wanted to get to know her more.

"Lord give me a sign," I said to myself. I wanted to know if this was real or was it just my head being fucked up from all the shots I took.

Lala was bouncing that fat ass to T.I.'s *Mediocre.* I had to agree that that song was all Lala, nothing was mediocre about her sexy ass. Just as that ass had a nigga tuned in like an episode of Love and Hip Hop, I saw James' bitch ass grab Lala's arm and tried to pull her off the dance floor.

The Indian looking girl she came with got in James' face. *Damn you work fast;* I thought to myself as I looked up to the ceiling. This was the sign I needed. I usually never put my cape on and played the role of Captain Save A Hoe, but that wasn't a hoe. I felt something for her.

Putting my hand on my waist to make sure my fie was there in place, I made my way to the dance floor. Bear and the other fellows peeped what was up, so they followed behind me like soldiers getting ready for war.

"Do we have a problem here?" I asked cocking my head to the side as I looked James square in the eyes. This nigga was mad pathetic.

"Nothing over here concerns you partna!" he replied, returning my gaze. Oh, so this nigga had big cow balls!

"Ms. Lala, are you ok?" I asked her. I could see the tear stains on her face. Putting two and two together, I did the math and realized that this cat was her man.

"Nigga, she alright! Let's go Lala now!" he yelled, snatching her by her hand again causing her to stumble and fall. *WHAM!* I punched that nigga right in the face. I don't know what came over me, but that shit had me livid! He got up to try to square up with me, but Lala got in between us.

"C'mon James, let's go," she whispered, looking down at the floor. Watching them walk towards the entrance together fucked my head up.

"You good?" Bear asked noticing the hurt in my eyes. I was fucked up about lil' mama for real though. She had me feeling shit that I ain't felt in a long time. A part of me wanted to walk out behind them and blast that nigga.

"Yeah, that was that nigga James," I said through gritted teeth.

"So, what you want me to do?" Bear asked with his hand on his piece ready to set it off.

"Nothing for now. I'm going to take his money, take over his city, and then take his girl. If that nigga got a problem, then I'll pump straight lead in his ass!" I replied, pulling the blunt from behind my ear.

"No doubt," Bear replied rolling up some Rainbow Kush that we copped from the Africans. This was that good shit a nigga from Africa name Aliba was growing. This shit didn't hit the streets yet, so I know money was going to start coming in by the boatload.

"This that good shit" Bear choked. I took a long toke, held it in my system, and let it out.

A few blunts and bottles later, a nigga was feeling like fucking something. I had ended up meeting a bitch name Katrina, she wasn't no Lala, but she wasn't ugly either. She was sitting on my lap swinging her red weave from side to side and bouncing her ass up and down. She turned around straddling me, looking me in my eyes while opening her legs wide showing me she ain't have no panties on underneath her dress.

I slid two fingers in her pussy and she started grinding on them as if it was a dick. She reached under her and pulled my dick out. Then the hoe got on all fours and started sucking my dick in the club. I shook my head. All the thoughts I had of bringing her to the hotel and banging her guts in flew out the window. There was no way in hell I was going to fuck a bitch that had no shame in sucking my dick in the club. My boy Bear looked over to me and gave me that "pass that hoe over here" look. After I pulled my dick out her mouth and nutted all on her face, that was exactly what I did.

The next morning, I woke up with a mean ass headache and with Lala on my mind. I took two extra strength Tylenols and grabbed my phone to text her.

Me: *You good ma?*

I laid back down in my California King sized bed and admired my room. The realtor my pops hooked me up with was bad! She had me in this four-bedroom three-bathroom house that sat on South Beach. I had my grandma fly down to decorate my house for me and it was looking nice.

I made sure no one knew where I lived. I never shitted where I laid my head. That was what fucked me up in the game the first time and I was not going to let that happen to me again. My phone chimed letting me know I had a text.

Lala: *I'm ok, thanks for asking. You?*

Me: *Just a little hangover, but I'll live.*

Lala: *Lol. I have to get ready for class, ttyl.*

I put my phone down and got out of bed to get my day started.

Today I was feeling like a boss, so I decided to push my all black Audi A4. Dressed in some Khaki polo cargos, a teal blue polo shirt, and some teal blue and khaki loafers, I decided to check in on a few of my traps.

I made my way to the Pork and Beans project where I was running a trap in a lady name, Ms. Lattie's, house. She was a sweet old lady that was about her money, so I used her house and a few of her other elder ladies friend's houses around the project to prevent my shit from getting raided. The chances of the law fucking with some old ladies who baked cookies, knit blankets, and went to church four times a week was slim to none.

"Hey baby!" Ms. Lattie greeted me with a kiss as soon as I walked through the door. She was sitting on her plastic couch in her nightdress and house shoes watching Maury. "I knew that nigga wasn't the father." She jumped up and down with the audience as soon as Maury read the results. "Don't cry now heffa, you wasn't crying when you was on that dick," she said with her hands on her hips. All I could do was shake my head and laugh at this old thug.

"I came to drop off your money and to check on things," I said pulling an envelope out my back pocket and handing it to her.

"Thank you baby, you hungry. I was just getting ready to fix breakfast," she asked me as she stuffed the envelope in her bra. Ms. Lattie was a cute heavyset old lady. Her son was one of the soldiers I had on my team. She was genuinely a sweet lady. That was why I always made sure I gave her a little extra money.

"No ma'am I'm fine, thanks for asking though," I replied, kissing her on her plump, rosey red cheeks. I made my way to the basement where I had one of my shops set up.

I saw Taz, a lil nigga that I had looking over this trap in the corner counting money while putting rubber bands around stacks. I was impressed; this young nigga was only seventeen and he was running shit like he was a grown ass man. I kept this nigga under my wing because he reminded me a lot of myself. I wanted him ready, so I was slowly molding him. His time was coming soon and he ain't even know it.

"What's good Taz?" I said, putting stacks of money in a duffle bag

"Nun boss, just coolin' it, getting this paper," he said never taking his eyes off the money

"I feel you kid, tight work boy." Giving him a nod of approval, I went to check on the rest of the niggas. I had Ms. Lattie basement set up in different sections. I had a few chicks cutting up and bagging dope in one corner. I had a few of my boys packaging them for me, and then I had Taz in his corner by himself counting my money. I had four ruthless bodyguards overseeing shit. Any wrong move and they had my permission to RIP that ass!! Shoot first; ask question later was the motto I lived by.

After I made my stops and picked up money from all my traps, I decided to hit up Bear and see what was good on his end. He was in Fort. Lauderdale looking after my setup that I had down there.

"What's good my nigga?" Bear greeted me.

"Nothing much, what's good in the Dale?" I asked him honking my horn at a crack head that ran in front of my car.

"Everything A-1 on this end. When you coming through?" he asked.

"I probably come down there later on today. Bear, let hit you up later, somebody on my line." I hung up. Looking at Lala's number flashing across my phone's screen, gave me butterflies. "What's good ma?" I answered the phone trying to add a little Keith Sweat to my voice.

"Can you meet me somewhere?" she whimpered into the phone. I could tell she'd been crying. I quickly gave her the address to my house and told her to meet me there. I knew I could be possibly putting myself in danger giving the nigga that I'm beefing with girl my address and shit, but fuck it. My head was gone already off Lala.

Two hours later, I was showered and waiting for her to come. I was starting to think this was a set up for real because she never showed up or called. Just as I was about to pick up the phone to order some take out, I heard a knock at the door. I went to open it; there was the most beautiful woman in the world standing right there before me.

Lala was wearing a green and black PINK sweat suit. Her hair was in a messy bun sitting on the top of her head. Her beautiful toes was painted and looking nice in a pair of black MK sandals. She looked so cute and professional with her glasses on.

She was amazingly beautiful and there wasn't an ounce of makeup on her face, flawless. I stepped to the side and let her in. She stood there looking at my living room. It was decorated in black and white. I had a black sectional with black and white throw pillow on it.

In the middle of the living room was a crystal glass table with a crystal bowl filled with black and white marbles. On the wall, there were pictures of my mom, grandma, Donna, and sonogram photos of my twins. A big painted portrait of Donna sat above the sectional. Above the fireplace was my 80-inch TV that I had mounted on the wall. I allowed her to walk through the living room looking through all the pictures. I watched her as she studied Donna's picture, then the twins.

"Your house is beautiful," she finally spoke after I silently gave her a tour of my house.

"Thanks, my grandma did her thing," I chuckled, hoping to make her feel comfortable. She sat on the couch looking down at the ground. I knew something was bothering her. Just her demeanor alone brought me to that conclusion. After what seemed like an hour of quietness, she burst out crying.

I went over the couch and held her in my arms as she cried. I knew that nigga wasn't treating her right. Instead of bringing this diamond to our meeting the first time we met, he decided to come with a rhinestone.

Her hair smelled like fresh flowers, her body was so soft; I had to mind trick my dick into staying down. I snapped back in reality after being lost in my infatuation with her and noticed that she was sleep. I carried her upstairs to my room and gently placed her body on my Michael Kors black, white, and gray bedding sheets.

I pulled the comforter back, gently took of her shoes, and covered her body. I took one last look at her and went down to my weight room to blow off some steam. She had me wanting to beat the pussy up in the worst way.

Meek Mills' *I'm Rollin'* was booming through the speakers in my weight room as I pumped iron. I was thinking irrationally, so I needed to lift weight to ease my mind. I was sexually frustrated. I wanted to pump five in to James' dome, I was missing Donna, my mom, and my twins. I had so much built up disgruntlement that I was going ham in the weight room.

Taking a swig of the bottle of water that was down by my foot, I looked up and noticed Lala standing the doorway. I hit the power button on the stereo.

"I hope I didn't wake you," I said, getting up and reaching for the towel.

"No I been up, just watching the show," she chuckled trying to lighten the mood.

"You hungry? I was about to make dinner," I said hoping that she would stay.

"Can you really cook or do I have to have a fire extinguisher on standby?" she joked.

"Nah, ma you good. You're looking at Chef-Boy-R-Nigga right here," I said flexing. We both laughed and it felt good to see that pretty smile on her face.

"Ok in that case, yeah, I can eat. Do you mind if I take a shower?" The thought of her in my shower naked had my dick doing the "Nae Nae" dance in my pants.

"Sure go ahead. The towels are in the linen closet next to the bathroom," I said trying not to sound excited. She nodded her head and walked out of the room. My eyes were zoomed in on her ass as she made her exit. Damn lil' mama had ass. I shifted my dick in my pants and drunk more cool water to quench the thirst I had for her.

"Something smells really good in here," Lala said walking into the kitchen in a pair of my boxers and one of my tank tops. I could see her nipples looking me in the eyes through the material of the tank. Her ass filled out my boxers real nice, had me wishing my name was Hanes. "I hope you don't mind. I didn't have anything to wear, so I borrowed these," she said noticing me admiring how sexy she looked in something so simple.

"Nah ma, you good, dinner will be ready in a little bit. Make yourself at home." She walked over to where I was standing and started looking through the pots.

"Smells and look good. I can't wait," she smiled and walked to the dining room table taking a seat at the cherry oak table. I swear that ass had a mine of its own; it was forever jiggling.

I sat two plates of pineapple-glazed salmon on a bed of white rice, with a side of lemon seared asparagus down on the table. We ate for the first five minutes in silence. All that could be heard was the forks hitting the plates and our mouth chomping down on the food.

"This is really good!" she moaned, putting a fork filled with salmon and rice in her mouth.

"I got skills," I smiled, winking at her and letting her know that I was that nigga.

"Who taught you how to cook so well?" she asked as she took a sip of her red wine.

The question threw me off a little. I learned how to cook from Donna. She was a chef and she basically taught me all that I knew. We used to cook up a storm in the kitchen together.

"Donna," I faintly answered. That was a very touchy subject for me and I didn't really feel ready to talk about it yet. I looked Lala in the eyes; damn she was just so beautiful to me. I wondered was what I was feeling for her real or was it just that I wasn't really ready to move on yet.

"So, are you going to tell me what I happened?" I asked not wanting her to pry more into the Donna subject.

"I just needed to get away from James and clear my head. Plus I really enjoy your company," she replied, shifting in her seat.

"You deserve better," I told her before finishing up the rest of my food. I had to stuff more food in my mouth to stop me from what I really wanted to say. I wanted to tell her to drop that lame ass nigga and come fuck with a real one.

"What makes you say that?" she questioned.

"Because I can tell you're not happy. I see it all in your face. You're too smart and beautiful to be allowing a nigga to treat you bad ma'," I replied back to her while downing the rest of my Hennessey.

"How do you know I'm not happy?" she asked, pouring herself another glass of red wine.

"If you were happy you wouldn't be here."

The room grew silent as she gazed into my eyes trying to ready my thoughts. If she was Ms. Cleo she would have known that I was feeling her to the max and all I wanted to do was step in and do everything that James couldn't. A part of me didn't feel ready, but fuck it, Donna was gone and no matter how much I prayed or how many niggas I killed, she was never coming back to me. I would never have the honor of holding my kids. All I had was memories that I could only cherish.

"Well, since you cooked it's only right that I clean the kitchen," she said breaking the silence.

"You sure?"

"Yeah, shooo fly I got this," she smiled as she started clearing the table. I watched her ass jiggle in my boxers before heading upstairs for a much needed cold shower.

I stood in the bathroom in my birthday suit preparing to take a shower. I adjusted the knobs to make sure the water was ice cold, I had to calm my right hand man down. I grabbed my Dove's Men body wash and began soaping up my body. Thoughts of Donna immediately started to flood my mind.

Lord please let her be the one to fill this void in my heart. Donna please forgive me for finally moving on. No matter what I will always love you and I am still going to avenge you and my shorties' deaths; I silently spoke to God and Donna.

If this was my second chance at love, I wasn't fucking it up. After I was sure that every part of my body was nice and clean, I got out the shower. Whipping the fog off the glass, I grabbed my toothbrush and brushed my teeth. With my towel wrapped around my waist, I walked into my room with Lala laying in my bed underneath the sheets watching 'Paid In Full' on Netflix.

"I hope you don't mind, I love this movie," she said never taking her eyes off the TV screen.

"Nah, you good. Make yourself at home, Ma'." I grabbed a pair of boxers, sweats, a tank top, and was about to make my way out the room to get dressed.

"You can get dress in here if you want. I don't want to feel like I'm putting you out of your own room," she smiled, finally looking my way. I saw the lust in her eyes, however; I wasn't going to take it that far with her. I respected her, and if I slept with her now, she would regret it because she wasn't fully over James, but hey, if she wanted a show, I'd give her one.

I allowed the towel to drop and matched her gaze as I proceeded to dress. The way her jaw hung let me know that she was impressed by Jr. This 10-inches of pure thick cut Grade A meat had her jaw watering.

"You might as well sleep over it's getting late," I said, looking at her. "You can stay in here. I'll crash in one of my guest rooms across the hall, let me know if you need anything." I was about to walk out the room until she asked me to stay, so I got into bed with her and held her close. While we were laying in bed, I turned off the TV and hit the power button on my six CD changer stereo. I flipped through the CD's until I came across my Lil Boosie Mix. I put it on song number nine as I let the words to the Lil Boosie's song explain to her how I really felt.

Let me ease yo mind
bring you in my world
cause you done caught my eye
and you can be my baby girl
it gon be alright
it gon be alright
cause u can be my baby girl

I sung along with the lyrics of the song as I held her tight in my arms. All I wanted to do was take the pain away and be that man that could show her better. I wanted her to be the woman that could be my calm after the storm. I wanted to be in love again, and possibly become a father. All I needed for her to do was make up her mind on what it was that she wanted to do.

I knew dude wasn't treating her right by the way she had that ass all pushed up against my dick. I wasn't going to push her into making a decision; I was just going to show her how a real man was supposed to treat her. I quickly said my nightly prayers before sleep came to claim me over for the night.

The next morning I woke up, she was gone. I finally knew how it felt to be a 'hit it and quit it' except I ain't hit it. I got up to handle my business. I was pissed and hurt at the same time. I expressed myself to her and she got up and left without even saying goodbye. I quickly pushed her out my mind because today it was time to get to work. I had to drive down to Fort. Lauderdale to pick up my money, drop off some dope, but I really wanted to see how Bear was holding things down. My phone started to ring. My heart jumped thinking it was Lala and I quickly dashed towards it and answered it.

"Good morning, Nana," I greeted my grandma. I was happy to hear from her, but was kind of disappointed that it wasn't Lala.

"Good morning Anthony, I no hear from you long time." She tried to speak English, but it wasn't so good since she was born in Haiti and she had a heavy accent.

"I'm sorry Nana, I've just been busy," I said feeling bad my first lady was feeling like I was neglecting her.

"You too busy for me right," she asked with a hint of hurt in her voice.

"No, Nana I will never be too busy for my first love. How are you cherie? Did you get the money I sent to you?" I said, trying to cover my ass before Nana got to snapping on me in Creole.

"Yes baby, thank you very much. You no have to keep send me money, Anthony. I'm ok." I knew my grandma and grandpa was set because my pops made it his business to take care of them, but the man in me wouldn't feel right if I didn't send her money. "You come eat Thanksgiving at my house?" she asked me, sounding like I was never gonna hear the end of it if I told her no.

"Of course, Nana, no woman can cook better than you," I replied tryna make her feel good .

"Oh, thank you baby, but I got to go to the market, I call you later. Be careful baby I love you," she said, she quickly prayed for me in Creole like she always did before we ended our calls.

"I love you too, Nana," I said before hanging up the phone.

Getting ready for my drive to the Dale, I put on a pair of jeans, an orange shirt with a home depot smock that read, "*Hello, my name is Dave.*" I also had on a pair of orange and white air max. I jumped in a 2001 green Honda Accord I bought cash from a dealer and was heading towards I-95. I was bringing blue drugs and bringing back money. I did not need to bring any unnecessary heat to myself.

The last thing I needed was for twelve to pull me over and try to search my shit because I was a black young man looking like money. My phone beeped showing that I had a text. I clicked on the message icon and my heart dropped as I read the text from Lala.

Lala: *I'm sorry…*

That could have only meant that she decided to work some shit out with that busta ass nigga. I was a little hurt, but fuck it, if it was meant to be then we'll be together. But one thing for sure I wasn't chasing no bitch that was stuck on stupid for a nigga.

Chapter 8

Bear

"Oh shit! Damn girl suck this dick." This bitch was putting in work! Her pussy was lame, but her head game was stupid. She swallowed my dick and I promise you I almost screamed like a little bitch. A few minutes later, she was sucking the head of my dick as I shot my load down her throat. "Tight work, Tasha, but check it you gotta clear it. That nigga Stacks on his way," I said picking her clothes off the ground and throwing them at her.

"Man fuck Stacks, you need to do what we came down here to do before he figure out it was you who killed Donna," Tasha snapped, smacking her lips.

"I need a little more time. I know that nigga seeing big money and as soon as I can get my hands on it then we good. We will be set for life baby. Now go before he sees you here." Tasha put on her clothes and walked out the door.

After killing that hoe Donna and robbing that nigga blind, I had enough money to get out of town, but when that nigga hit me up and said he needed me down here to look after his operation, the greed in me decided to get his ass again. The first time around I had my girl Tasha fucking with Stacks as a distraction. I paid attention to that nigga's every move and waited for the perfect opportunity to attack.

Stacks and I had been boys for a long time, but as soon as he found out that his dad was this big cartel dude, shit changed. I envied him when he went to Columbia and came back smelling like money. I was livid. I hated the fact that he was handed everything I worked so hard for. I wanted the fame and fortune he had in these streets and from that point on, I began thinking of a master plan.

Operation "Take Stacks Down". So, yeah I robbed that nigga and fucked Donna fine ass for a week straight before I killed her ass. I convinced him it was these niggas out West that we was beefing with. I even went as far as to making one of the niggas from the West confess that it was him and his crew that raided his house.

I sat and watch as Stacks tortured that little nigga while looking for more information. The day Stacks threatened to go for his family, he decided that the money wasn't worth it. When I got the feeling that he was gonna talk and blow my spot up, I killed his ass. Stacks thought I was his right hand, but in reality, I was a snake in disguise.

A knock at the door snapped me out of my thoughts. I got up and made sure there were no traces of Tasha before I opened the door.

"What's up my nigga?" I greeted Stacks as soon he walked through the door.

"What you stopped hustling and got you a job at The Home Depot?" I joked.

"Nah, nigga I ain't tryna bring no heat my way. So, how business going down here?" he asked, taking a seat on the couch.

"Business is going good," I replied handing him a five duffle bags filled with money.

"That's what's up. C'mon let's ride, so I can show face at these trap houses." We got up, headed out the door and got in my Pontiac G6. We were on our way to the East where I had my lil set up and trap houses. We went through each of the trap and Stacks was quiet as he watched me interact with my workers. He was on some inspection type shit by the way he was nodding and mentally taking notes.

"Ayo Bear that nigga Red is short 800 dollars," one of my workers name, Ted, told me. I did not need this shit right now.

"Fuck man, bring that nigga here," I snapped. I was pissed. Out of all the fucking days these niggas could fuck up, they decided to do it while Stacks was here.

An hour later, Ted and Red walked through the door.

"Boss man I'mma have yo' money by the end of the week," he stammered, sounding like a little bitch.

WHAM!

Stacks hit his ass with a two-piece.

"When you fuck with his money, you fuck with my money and when you fuck with my money, I get pissed" Stacks said to Red. His voice was so calm, but it held so much authority. He still looked like a boss even though he was dressed like a Home Depot employee. That shit instantly pissed me off. I wanted so badly to turn my pistol on him and body his ass. I had to get my emotions in check and remind myself his time was going to come soon.

After all that, we chopped it up on the block, smoked a little weed, and Stacks was on his way back to Miami. I was glad to see that nigga gone. I had enough of pretending for the day. As soon as he was gone, I called up Tasha and asked her ass to meet me at the house. We had to put this plan in motion and I knew exactly whom we could team up with.

Chapter 9

James

My stress level was on ten. First, I was having problems with wifey, then my connect all of a sudden disappeared on me. I knew that nigga Stacks had something to do with it. Ever since that nigga decided came to Miami, he'd been nothing but a pain in my ass. He was fucking with my money and was trying to get at my bitch. Anybody who knew me, knew that those were two things that I ain't play about.

"What we going to do about this nigga?" Nico said, passing me the blunt.

"He wants war, we going to bring his ass war!" I replied before I took a long pull of the joint. I held the Kush in longer. Damn! This nigga had my pockets running dry. My phone beeped and I looked down at it and I had two texts; one from Lala and the other from Ashley. I opened the one from Lala first.

Wifey: *Bae where you at?*

Me: *Chillin' with Rico, Why What's up.* I replied and scrolled down to Ashley's text and read it.

"SHIT!" I said out loud after reading her text. Rico looked over to me trying to figure out what was wrong. I grabbed the blunt from his hand and tossed the phone in his lap. He picked up the phone and read the text.

"Damn son," he said, shaking his head. As soon as my phone beeped he handed it back to me.

Wifey: *I was wondering if we could go to dinner and a movie.*

Me: *I'mma be making runs all night bae, how about you and Lisa go out. I'll make it up to you later.*

Wifey: *yeah ok.*

I felt bad neglecting my girl especially when we were working things out, but I had to get to the bottom of this shit with Ashley.

In CVS, I picked up one of each of the different brand of pregnancy test there was, and then made my way to Ashley's house. A part of me was happy because I was dying to have a seed, but no matter how many times I came in Lala, she never ended up pregnant. The fact that Lala was my girl and Ashley was my side bitch immediately fucked my head up. How was I going to explain this shit to Lala?

I put my key in the door and walked in the house. Ashley was sitting down on the ground crying.

"Oh, my God James. I don't know how this happened," she cried. A part of me felt bad for putting her in this fucked up situation. I handed her the bag, she looked in side of it, and walked to the bathroom to pee on the sticks.

Those three minutes felt like three years. I looked down at the counter where she laid the tests in a row; all those motherfuckers said yes. My jit was in her.

"I can get rid of it," she innocently said, looking down at the ground.

"Dead that thought, you ain't killing my fucking child!" I yelled, swiping all the tests off the counter and knocking them to the ground. The thought of her killing my first child fucked my head up. I was mad at myself for being so careless, but I would never take that anger out on my seed. I poured myself a glass of Remy, went and sat on the couch, and rolled a blunt. Lala was the only thing on my mind. We just got back on good terms now here I was fucking up again.

Ashley came in the living room and handed me a plate of brown stew chicken with some peas and rice. I wasn't really that hungry, so I declined it. I got up and went to the room to go lay down. A part of me wanted to go home to Lala and take her on that date, but my mind was too fucked up.

The only thing that came to my mind was trying to hide it all from her. I couldn't lose my girl over this shit. I had to have a talk with Ashley too; it was time to dead this little affair. I battled with my thoughts until sleep took over me.

Chapter 10

Ashley

Operation get pregnant was a success. I had to play the victim role so he wouldn't suspect that I did this on purpose. Now that I almost had my man, I had to make sure our futures were secured. Stacks was out there running my man's streets and eating all the food off our plates.

It was going to come to an end soon because I had something for his ass. I called my cousin Ted up. He was telling me how his boss wanted to meet with James on some get money type shit. I knew James would be mad at me for getting in his business, but to hell with that. We were about to bring a baby in this world and I was not about to be sitting at no damn welfare office. After my phone conversation with Ted, I went upstairs to lie down next to my man.

The next morning, I woke up to James rubbing my tummy. I knew getting pregnant would warm his heart.

Ever since I met him, he'd always talked about him and Lala having a baby.

"Did I wake you?" he asked me, still rubbing my stomach.

"No," I replied, loving this feeling.

"You hungry?" he asked, sitting up in the bed.

"Yeah I.." I couldn't even finish my sentence before I made a 5-yard dash to the bathroom. I threw up for what seemed like hours. I sat on the bathroom floor trying to catch my breath.

"You good?" James asked as he handed me a bottle of water. I drunk it all down in one gulp, only to have my head right back in the toilet bowl throwing it all up.

"You need me to get you anything?" he asked as he grabbed a washcloth, wet it and handed it to me.

"Some tea and crackers would be good." I was out of breath. This little bastard was already getting on my bad side. I brushed my teeth and headed back to bed.

"Where you going?" I asked James as he got dressed.

"Home. I'll be back later," he said as he grabbed his keys and was out the door. Something had to fucking give! I was sick of that nigga running back to that bitch!

I haven't heard from Loye in a minute so I decided to call up my diva.

"What's T fish?" Loye answered, sounding out of breath.

"Damn hoe, what you was doing?" I quizzed.

"Nothing boo, just got off the treadmill, you know I gotta keep this body looking right," he said, sounding like he was drinking something.

"I know that's right," I co-signed.

"How's my God baby doing?" he asked.

"Man this little bastard got me throwing up and shit. If it wasn't for its daddy, my ass would have been right at the clinic!" I listened as Loye laughed his ass off.

"Hey you wanted it, so deal with it."

"I know," I sadly stated. For the first time, I realized that I was about to be somebody's mother. I wasn't ready to have a baby. I loved partying, drinking, and living my carefree life. I had to hurry up with my plan, so I could get rid of this baby before it was too late.

Concocting a new plan in my head, I decided to log into Facebook. I typed Lala Williams in the search engine and her page popped up. I was happy that her page wasn't on private. I went through her post and one in particular caught my attention. She just posted it three minutes ago and it read; *My baby just came home with flowers, getting ready to go out and have breakfast with my hubby by the beach. #TeamJames*

I was furious! I was the one carrying this nigga's first child, but he was taking the next bitch out. I decided to make a fake page. I had some pictures of my old roommate. I uploaded them and named my page Keyshia Daniels. I also took my time perfecting a photo-shopped picture of her and James and uploaded that, as well.

I sent a whole bunch of her friends and random people friend request. Then I sent her one. I made sure to have that photo-shopped picture as the profile pic, so she wouldn't second-guess on accepting the friend request. To put the icing on the cake, I uploaded a few post about us being together. I smiled at my handy work and went to make myself something to eat.

***

My meeting with Ted and Bear was at 2:15 and it was already 1:45 and I was stuck on the I in this bad ass traffic. It was 2:30 when I finally pulled up to the address that was sent to me in a text. I stepped out my car and walked to the door.

"What's up cuz?" Ted greeted me as he opened the door for me.

"Nothing, just chilling. Sorry I'm late, but that traffic ain't no joke," I said making my way in the house. I saw this Rick Ross look alike sitting next to the prettiest dark skinned girl I'd ever seen.

"Yo fam, this my cousin Ashley I was talking about. Ayo Ash, this Bear and his girl Tasha," Ted said introducing us.

"What's good?" Bear greeted me, licking his lips. I could feel his eyes burning holes through my shorts, probably figuring out how I got all this ass in them.

"Where yo' nigga James at?" he asked still eye fucking me.

"He don't know what's going on, and he don't have to. I'm just ready to put the necessary work in to eliminate the threat," I spoke up, licking my full lips right back at him. Hell if he wanted to act sexually, I could too.

"I hear you," he nodded.

"What's in it for you?" he asked me.

"Well, I was hoping to kill two birds with one stone. I want to get rid of Stacks because he's the cause of my man's pockets going dry. In exchange, you help me eliminate a threat to my family," I said putting it all on the table.

"And who might that be?" He sat up looking me directly in my eyes, probably trying to figure out if I was really about that life.

"James' bitch, Lala," I smirked and leaned forward. I made sure he had a view of my breast. I heard his bitch suck her teeth, but I didn't give a fuck. I'd drop my panties right now and jump on his dick right in front of her face. She must ain't know I was that bitch.

We sat down and perfectly strategized how to take Stacks down. Bear would continue to act like he was working for him. They would hit their own trap houses making it look like somebody was on that beef shit. Once Stacks let Bear in to where he had enough information, we'd use it against him to bring him down. This time permanently and six feet under. There was no way we were going to allow him a third chance. I wanted to live.

James called me a few times during our meeting so as soon as I got to my car, I decided to return his call.

"Why the fuck you wasn't picking up the phone?" he snapped as soon as he answered the phone.

"I was having lunch with Loye and I left my phone in the car," I quickly lied, trying to diffuse the situation.

"Ok, so when you coming home?"

Hearing the word 'home' had me cheesing. He considered my house 'home' and I wanted to make sure it stayed that way, even if I had to commit murder. Hell, I made up my mind to kill the lil' bastard in me, so killing Lala's bitch ass would be a piece of cake.

"I'll be there in a little bit bae," I heard my phone click, signaling that he hung up on me.

Before driving off, I decided to check on my fake page. I logged in as 'Keyshia Daniels' and saw that Lala accepted my friend request, so I decided to have some fun. I saw that she was online, so I sent her a message.

"Hey, my name is Keyshia and I want to come to you woman to woman to let you know that James and I have been together for two years now. I was not aware that you two were together until I came across your page through our mutual friends.

I am very hurt that James would do this to me. He proposed to me and all. I had to cut him loose after I found out how wrong he was doing us. Please let him know to go get tested. That dirty bitch gave me Trichomoniasis. I'm so done with him.

Please have him come pick up his things off the curb before the garbage man come and pick them up for him. Once again, I am truly sorry for coming at you like this, but that nigga ain't shit."

I laughed out loud as I sent the message. I waited a few minutes to see if she was going to reply to me, but instead she just read it and logged off. Either way, I didn't care. It was only a matter of time before both of my problems would be gone.

Chapter 11

Lala

I got off the phone with the clinic after making my appointment. To say I was pissed was an understatement. I was done with this nigga for real. Here, I had a nigga that was ready to do right by me and I was still stuck on James' dog ass. I packed all my things and put my luggage in the trunk of my car.

Good thing he was not here because I would have ended up going to jail for murder. After eight years of my life, all the sacrifices I made for him and he repays me back with a fucking STD.

After I had all of my things packed, I grabbed the two-gallons of bleach I had in the laundry room. I gathered all of his shoes, clothes, hats, jewelry; all of it and put them in the tub where I poured the bleach all over his shit. When I was done taking out my anger on all of his most prized possessions, I decided to leave. I took the house key off my key ring and left it on the table.

I drove around for two hours and then ended up in front of Stacks' house. My mind was yelling at me telling me that this was a bad idea and to turn around and go to Lisa's house, but I ignored it. I popped my trunk and carried all my luggage to his front porch. I stood there for a moment not sure on how he would react.

We hadn't talked since that day he basically told me how he felt and I left him high and dry. I shrugged it off and decided to take a chance. I rang his doorbell and immediately regretted it. What if he had a girl in there? I picked up my bags to walk away and that's when I heard the door open.

"You still with the games I see?" Stacks said as came out the door in his basketball shorts only. Oh, goodness his chest was beautiful. He grabbed the luggage out my hand and I followed him inside. For some reason, I felt comfortable around him. I was even feeling him, too. I didn't feel like talking so I went upstairs and climbed in his bed. All I wanted was for him to hold me like he did the other night and that was exactly what he did, he held me, and I cried.

"I'm ready to let you ease my mind," I softly said before sleep took over me.

***

The next morning, I woke up to an empty bed and the smell of cinnamon. I went downstairs and was shocked. Stacks had a breakfast laid out with fresh flowers everywhere.

"Good morning," he said poring two glasses of orange juice.

"Morning, this is beautiful." I blushed as he handed me a single red rose.

"Not as beautiful as you," he smiled, showing off those dimples that I loved so much. "I didn't know what you like to eat, so I made a variety of things," he said, pulling some honey biscuits from the oven. I sat down at the table and piled my plate with eggs, cheese grits, fried tilapia, and biscuits.

"So you want to tell me what happened," he said as he sipped his orange juice while looking at me.

"It's a long story," I said trying to end the subject.

"I got time," he seriously stated.

"I'm done with James. I decided to leave him. He was dating this girl name Keyshia behind my back for over a year. All the days that he spent away from home handling "business" was him living his double life. It's only so much a woman can take. I just decided to come here because I knew that Lisa's house would be the first place he'd come looking for me. I promise not to stay long, I'll be gone after breakfast." Biting down on my lip, I tried not to cry, but this was too much for me. How could someone you love so much hurt you so bad?

"Why would he do this to me? Am I not pretty enough, what am I doing so wrong?" I sobbed not able to hold back anymore.

"Listen to me ma, you are beautiful. You are an amazing woman. Don't even let a man make you feel unsure of yourself. He wasn't man enough to treat you right. It takes a king to handle a queen and he was nothing but a joker." He pulled me in his arms and held me. For the first time in a long time, I felt secure.

***

"When do you go back to work?" Stacks asked as he walked into the room where I was studying.

"I decided to take my vacation early, so in two weeks," I answered, looking up from my Adult Health II book that I was studying from.

"Cool, you got any plans for today?" he asked, picking up my Trauma book and started flipping through the pages.

"No, just pretty much studying that's all. You?" I asked as I noticed him put the book down and grab a pair of blue, green, and black Adidas to put on.

"I'm on my way out to make some rounds, but I'll be home in time to take you out to dinner." He winked at me before putting on his blue and black fitted cap.

"Sounds like a plan," I said, smiling. For some reason when I was with Stacks he made me feel things I shouldn't be feeling. I was still very much in love with James, but my feelings for Stacks were slowly creeping up on me.

"Girl, where the fuck are you?" Lisa yelled in my ear. "Do you know James came over here banging on my door and 5 a.m. asking for you!!" she vented. I could tell she was mad. She hated not knowing what was going on and by the sound of the voicemails she left, I decided to call her to let her know that I was ok.

"I'm good bestie, I just decided to detour to Stacks' house. I knew he was going to come looking for me over there," I replied, examining my nails. Damn, I was in need of a fill.

"Ooooh chyyy, let me find out you done got you a new man," she laughed, being real extra.

"It's not even like that, Lisa, he is different on so many levels. I think I'm feeling him a little bit," I half told the truth. I was really feeling Stacks.

"Good! Now, you can finally get over that no good ass nigga!" she snapped, popping her gum.

"It's easier said than done." I felt my heart slowly crumbling at the thought of James and I finally ending.

"Well, you need to figure out what you're going to do. It is not good to stay and play with Stacks' emotions if you're only going to run back to that dog. It is time you move on. How many more tears do you have to cry? It's a possibility that he may have given you a STD. What's are you waiting on? Him to give you AIDS? Grow up ma' for real," Lisa lectured.

Sometimes I wished I was as strong minded as she was. She didn't take shit from no nigga. If only I had an ounce of her confidence, I'd be good.

"Yeah, you right." I didn't want to agree with her, but she was right. I loved my life too much to catch AIDS behind a nigga that didn't give a fuck about his own life. If he gave a fuck about our health, he wouldn't be out here bare backing random hoes. Lisa and I chopped it up a bit before we ended our call. As soon as I put my phone down, it started beeping signaling that I had a text message.

James: *This how we do it now?*

I started not to reply to his text, but I decided to put him out of his misery.

Me: *James I'm done!!! Please leave me alone or I will seriously block you.*

James: *Bae why you doing this to me. I don't know who the fuck this Keyshia is I swear to God!*

Me: *Goodbye James.*

Tossing my phone on the couch, I decided to get up and get ready. I had an appointment today and I was nervous. I usually was on top of these things since I was a med student and I worked in the health field; however, I put my trust in this stupid ass nigga!

Walking past a few pictures, I studied Donna. She was real pretty, the glow in her face, and the way she smiled at her tummy made me realize that I wanted more in life. I didn't just want to be somebody's "girlfriend" or "baby mama", I wanted to be a "wife". I looked at a few more of her pictures thinking if I was ready to jump into something new with Stacks. Hell, I didn't even know if he was fully over his ex.

I looked at more pictures of Donna and started second guessing the whole thing until I felt something. Call me crazy, but I swear I felt my heart answer for me. I let my thoughts take control of me for a few more minutes before I decided to go and get ready for my appointment.

The drive to Homestead was two hours. I didn't want to chance running into anyone I knew, so I decided to drive to the furthest clinic.

"Hi, how can I help you?" the chubby white nurse asked me with all the attitude in the world in her voice. The way I was feeling I was bound to smack her ass.

"Yes, I have an appointment at three," I politely stated, giving her the biggest smile ever. Sometimes the only thing you could do for rude people was to kill their asses with kindness.

"Fill this out and wait to be called," she said, handing me a clipboard stacked with paperwork. I took a seat on one of the plush seats they had in the waiting room and began taking in the scenery. It was a really nice, cozy doctor's office. The floor was marble and buffed to perfection, the cream chairs were a nice color to match the brown and red color scheme they had going on.

There were posters of different quotes on the wall and big baskets filled with condoms in every section of the room. My phone beeped, snapping me back to reality. I quickly glanced at the text and began filling out the forms. *How many sex partners have you had in the past year?* I quickly filled in one. I bet James ass probably wouldn't be able to answer that question with his hoe ass. I filled out everything and waited to be called. A small tear slid down my face; I was truly hurt by James' actions. All these years and this is my repayment.

"B-64 to room number four," I heard someone say through an intercom. I sat there still looking around until my eyes fell on a small, blue card that had that number on it. I got up and made my way to door number four. At the desk sat a handsome, older man. His baldhead glistened as if he just shinned it.

His salt and pepper goatee was perfectly trimmed. His skin was a smooth dark chocolate, he reminded me of an older version of Morris Chestnut.

"Have a seat," he said, sizing me up and down. I followed his eyes down to my legs and I could tell he was in awe at how nice they looked in my 6-inch pumps. I walked over to the chair, sat down, and crossed my legs seductively. I LMAO in my head when he cleared his throat, sat up, and adjusted his tie. "I'm Dr. Anderson. What brings you in today, Ms. Williams?" he asked obviously enticed by my beauty.

"Well a young lady that was engaging in sexual activities with my ex-boyfriend said she contracted Trich," I answered, feeling ashamed that I was in this position.

"Ok, so what I am going to do is give you an injection of antibiotics. Now this injection will cure all STIs except, Genital Herpes, Genital Warts, Hepatitis B, and HIV. I'm going to need you to go to room six and the nurse will prep you. It does take seven days for you to get your results back, you can either come in or call the number and provide them with the password you wrote down."

The doctor scribbled a few words down and escorted me to room six. The nurse swabbed my mouth, vagina, took blood, and then asked me to bend over a chair with my ass poking up in the air as if I was about to get dicked down. The doctor came in and stuck me in the ass with a needle and sent me on my way with a brown paper bag filled with condoms.

Chapter 12

Lisa

Lil Mamma gotta ass so fat, I ain't never seen it twerk like that, so when she turn around and work it, back it up and dump, ask her who she twerkin' for like that, she say she twerkin' it for daddy. V.I.C sang as I bounced my ass to the beat.

I grabbed the pole and slid down up side down while flipping in a split. I made my ass cheeks bounce to the beat. Left cheek, right cheek, left cheek. The niggas was going crazy and they were showing mad love. I untied my top, and pulled off my thong. I laid on my back, opened a Cherry Blow pop I pulled out of my ponytail, and plunged it deep in my pussy. I then walked up to one of the guys and stuck it in his mouth. Fives, tens, and twenties was being showered all over me as the crowd went crazy.

"Alright y'all show Seduction some love," the DJ said as I walked off the stage with all my money in tow. It never failed, even on slow nights, I was racking in dough. I was one of the baddest in this club.

This was my fucking life. I loved shaking my ass for money; it gave me a sense of power. Lala wanted to be a nurse and I wanted to be a certified stripper. We both started out stripping a while back. Lala walked away after she became a LPN, but me? I couldn't. The money was too good and the fame was even better.

Niggas from all over the world came to KOD to watch me shake my ass. I went to my locker, stashed my money in a little cut out compartment I had my mini safe in, and then locked it back up. These poor ass hoes would rob you blind in a heartbeat if they caught you slipping.

I grabbed my Summer's Eve Vaginal wipes and cleaned myself. I changed into my one-piece see through thong set. I laced up my stoned black 8-inch high heels with the 4-inch platform. After spraying my coochie with some Island breeze Summer's Eve vaginal spray, I was ready to walk the floor. I had to stay on point. Sweaty pussy don't make no money.

"Can I get a lap dance?" the Rick Ross lookalike asked me, He looked familiar, I just couldn't figure out where I seen him from.

"Sure," I licked my lips, leading him to one of the private rooms. T-Pain's *Up Down* started playing and I started bouncing my ass. When I saw the enormous stack of money sitting on the end table next to him, my eyes lit up like a kid on Christmas morning. My adrenaline started pumping. I put my body in a handstand position and flipped my body, so that I was straddling his lap.

"You like this daddy?" I moaned, licking his ear as I started grinding my pussy on his dick. He let his money answer for him; he popped the rubber band of the stack and made the whole thing rain on me. JACKPOT! As soon as the song finished, he left the room. I was too busy picking up my money to even notice him go.

I gave a few more lap dances and decided to call it a night. I packed my things and stuffed them in my Gucci book bag with all my earnings for the night. I made sure my pink chrome 9mm was secured on my hip. Fuck with me and I was going to send yo ass to meet the Devil with no hesitation. I said my goodbyes and made my way to my car.

"You shouldn't be walking to you car alone this late," a voice from behind me said. By reflex, I pulled out my 9 and pointed it in the mystery guy's direction. "Just chill Ma', I ain't trying to rob you," he laughed and came closer. It was the Rick Ross lookalike.

"Can I walk you to your car?" he asked, smiling and showing off them sexy ass golds.

"Yes, you can," I blushed. I wasn't normally a chubby chaser, but I'd fuck with him especially if he was really big banking.

"This you?" he said as I hit the alarm on my Beamer.

"Yes, it is," I smiled proud of my baby. I worked hard to get her and I paid her off cash, no payments.

"Damn ma if it's like that, then let me hold something?" he joked. Well, at least I hope he was joking because there was no way in hell I was giving this money back. His phone started ringing, he looked at it, and turned the ringer off. His bitch must be wondering where his ass was at. "Give me your phone," he said pinning me against my car while invading my personal space.

The smell of his cologne invaded my nostrils instantly putting me in a daze. I unlocked my phone and handed it to him. He put his number in my phone and saved it and then called himself so that he'd have mine, as well. He gave me my phone back and walked away. Yes you one sexy papa Bear, I thought looking down at his now saved number.

***

Punching in the code to my alarm, I made my way in the house. I was excited to count the money I made tonight. Dumping all the contents of my bag on the floor, I gathered all the money and started counting it. Thirty minutes and ten sore fingers later, I beamed with delight looking down at the 25,000 I made in less than five hours. Bitches working 9-5's was making this a year. I put half in the safe that I had built in the back of my headboard and saved the other half to split and put in my two bank accounts. Waiting on my TV dinner to finish, I decided to text my best bitch.

Me: *I know you probably sleep, just wanted to let you know that I love you. Good night babes!*

The microwave started beeping letting me know my dinner was ready. *Damn I need to invest in some cooking lessons*; I thought as I sat and ate the flavorless macaroni. I finished up my food, made sure my kitchen was cleaned, before retiring upstairs to bed. Whoever said shaking ass wasn't work lied. I was dog tired.

***

Yeah I love them strippers; yeah I love them strippers. My phone rang waking me out of my sleep. I was getting ready to snap on the person calling me at nine in the fucking morning until I saw Bear's name on the screen.

"Hello?" I answered, putting a hint of sexy in my voice.

"What's good ma, I hope I ain't wake you," he replied

"No you good, I been up," I lied, sitting up in my bed.

"I was wondering if I could take you out to dinner tonight if you don't mind," he said sounding like he was smoking.

"How you going to take me out and you don't even know my name?" I sassed trying to play hard to get.

"Why I don't Lisa?" he chuckled.

"How you know my name." I asked embarrassed.

"I know everything, you rolling with me or what?" he asked, bringing out his gangster.

"Yeah," I answered, not wanting to sound too excited.

"Bet, text me your address and I'll be there at 8 p.m." We said our see you laters and I got up to go shower. I had to get right for tonight.

"Hello," Lala answered sounding like she was still sleep.

"Bitch, get yo' ass up and meet me at Star Nails," I told her while pulling my tights over my ass.

"Ugh, give me am hour," she whined before hanging up in my ear. I seriously didn't know what I would do without Lala; she was truly my other half. My mom and dad both died in a car crash and she was the only one I had left. Yeah, I had two brothers, Jimmy and David, but with Jimmy in the Army and David in jail that left just me.

I loved Lala with all my heart and she was the only reason I ain't lullaby James' ass yet. But let me find out he slipped up and gave my girl something, I would be personally delivering his mother her black dress with the shoes to match.

***

Lala parked a clean ass Audi next to my car. Damn She was only living at this nigga Stacks' house for a week and she was already pushing a got damn 2014 Audi!!

"Damn bitch, you must be sucking the skin off that dick for you to be riding so clean," I joked, putting a fresh piece of Trident gum in my mouth.

"Shut up, it ain't even like that," she said.

"Then tell me what it's like," I quizzed, wanting to know how she got to push an Audi without even giving up the goods.

"My Lex caught a flat and he told me to grab one of his cars, that's all," she shrugged, walking into the salon and leaving me with my thoughts. I walked in behind her and we both sat in silence waiting to be called.

"I got a date tonight," I said as Ming Lee scrubbed my feet.

"With who?" Lala asked, looking at her nails. She was picky ass fuck. If it didn't look right, she'd soak them off and make the nail tech re-do them.

"Some guy I met at work, Bear." She looked at me as if that name sounded familiar and was trying to put a face to it.

"Bear?" she asked cocking and tilting her head to the side. "That name sounds familiar."

"His face look familiar, too," I told her, watching Ming apply the nude color polish to my toes. "But he's cute and girl I'm not going to tell you how he made it rain on me last night." I made a hand gesture as if I was making it rain.

"So, are you going to take him serious or is he going to be one of you tricks?" she asked knowing me all too well.

"We'll see. In other words, did you get your results back?" I seriously asked.

"Yeah, well no. I been too scared to call in." She looked at me like she was about to cry. At that moment, I wished I had my gun. I ain't play no games when it came to my bitch.

"Lala, just do it," I told her as I got up and walked over to the dryer section.

"Will you do it for me please?" she begged, giving me those puppy dog eyes.

We sat down at the drying table and she dialed the number. I clicked option two for the results hotline. After holding for nearly twenty minutes, an agent came to the phone. I impersonated Lala giving all of her information. The rep asked me for the security code and I told her green light. That was our code word we uses to use at the strip club whenever we needed back up. The lady read off the results. I thanked her, hung up the phone, and looked at Lala.

Chapter 13

Bear

Parking in front of lil' mama's house, I shot her a quick text letting her know that I was outside. I had to keep reminding myself that this was strictly business. I had to get in the bitch's head to get more information on Stacks. He already told me that her home girl had been crashing with him at his spot and since I ain't know where he laid his head, I had to use baby girl so that I could find out. I hated to do it to her because I could tell that she was feeling me, but money talks and bullshit walks a thousand miles. I just hope she didn't fall in love with a nigga.

When she walked out the door, all that not mixing business with pleasure quickly flew out the window. Lil' mama was bad! Her and Lala was indeed two of the baddest bitches I'd ever seen. My girl Tasha was bad, too, but she ain't have shit on them. She was looking sexy ass fuck in that crop top she had on. I was hoping she ain't have no panties on under that skirt.

"I hope I ain't keep you waiting long," she smiled as she got in my car.

"You good," I told her, making sure she was seated before backing out of the driveway and pulling off. I decided to take her to this nice little restaurant I spotted down by the beach next to Wet Willie's.

Once we got to our destination, I opened her door for her and placed my hand on the small of her back as we walked in. Yeah I was on my gentlemen type shit tonight. I was trying to get in good with shawty. As soon as we walked in, we were seated. We ordered our food, drinks, and had an enjoyable dinner. Her mind was on another level and I liked that. She was about her money and she had a hint of gangster in her. If I didn't have the motives of using her, I could see myself fucking with her like that.

We decided to grab a few drinks from Wet Willie's and sit on the beach. I purchased a few blankets from this small beach shop.

"I really enjoyed tonight," she said, taking off her shoes.

"Yeah, I did too ma'." I pulled her down on the blanket with me so that she was sitting in between my legs. In silence, we sipped on our drinks and watched the waves.

"So does this mean I get a second date?" I whispered in her ear, gently nibbling on it.

"Mmhmm," she moaned as I stuck my tongue in her ear. She turned around and started kissing me with so much passion I wanted to push her ass off me, but instead I pulled them panties to the side and played with her clit. Her breathing and moaning let me know that she was close to her peak, so I applied pressure on her clit and had her skirting all in my hand. She pushed me back on the blanket and undid my jeans. I felt her warm mouth swallow my dick.

"Oh damn!" I groaned as she worked the jaw muscles on my dick. The only bitch that could have me busting a nut off of head alone was Tasha, but right now she had Tasha beat in the head game.

Not wanting to go out like a bitch, I pulled out a condom from my back pocket and slid it on my dick. I lifted her up and placed her right on my dick. I saw her strip, so I knew she was good at riding a dick, at least I hoped she was. She slid up and down on my dick pulling me deep in her warmness. I done fucked up the moment I slid in this pussy. How was I gonna stop fucking with her? This now was going to become conflict of interest.

"Damn!" I moaned when she turned around on the dick and started riding me from the back. If it was a crime for having good pussy, she would have been given the electric chair.

"Oh shit daddy!!" she moaned before I felt her squirt on my dick. I lifted her up and down on my dick until we came together. We chilled for a little bit before I decided to bring her home. Once I got to her spot, she asked me if I wanted to come in and as tempting as that sounded, I had to decline. I was not trying to fall for her and shawty already had me on edge. Another hit of that pussy and I would of been gone for real.

***

"Did you fuck her?" was how Tasha greeted me as soon as I walked in the house.

"And if I did?" I asked, giving her ass the side eye.

"That wasn't apart of the fucking plan," she yelled, getting in my face.

"You fucked Stacks!" I shot back at her.

"You told me to!!" she screamed out making a valid point.

"I had to get in her head somehow. How the fuck else am I going to get the information I need from her? Going into this you knew there was a chance that I was going to fuck her, so I don't know why you acting like this," I said walking out the room.

I was sitting on the bed texting Lisa when Tasha came in the room. She got on her knees in front of me, pulled down my pants, and sucked my dick back to life. She paused, and then went back to sucking. I knew she could taste the latex on my dick confirming her suspicions, but that didn't stop her.

Usually, Tasha's head game would have a nigga gone, but all I could do was think about Lisa. She must have sensed that I wasn't into the head she was giving me by the way the tears were streaming down her face. She tried to go beast mode, but that only made my dick go limp. I got up leaving her there on her knees and went to go take a shower.

After my shower, I decided to go sleep in the guest room just so I could cake up with Lisa after Tasha went to sleep.

***

The following day, I decided that today was the day to put part of my plan in motion. I made a phone call to Stacks letting him know that we were robbed.

"What the fuck you mean a few of the trap houses got hit?" Stacks yelled through the phone. I had to keep myself from laughing knowing that I was the one behind it all. While I was out with Lisa last night, I had a few jack boys hit a few of the trap houses for me. I let them keep the drugs and I kept the money. Once Stacks got word that someone that wasn't from our crew was selling our shit, it would start a war. I needed a war to start to put my plan in full affect.

"Man I'm about to call a meeting right now. I'm killing all these niggas for being so damn careless with my shit," I said, putting on a show.

"Man, I'll be down there in a few hours," he replied before hanging up the phone. That nigga was mad as fuck.

Ted and I burst out laughing at that nigga.

"Fam, you one ruthless ass nigga," Ted said, passing me the joint.

"You ain't seen ruthless yet," I said, taking a pull on the joint. I was about to turn Stacks' life upside down and as soon as I found out where he was stashing the money and drugs it was asta la vista for that nigga. I planned on moving to a small island while collecting money from Ted who was going to stay down here and push weight for me. I had it all planned out; I just hoped that it worked out in my favor.

Chapter 14

Stacks

Not a-fucking-gain; I thought throwing the glass I held in my hand. I couldn't believe niggas wanted to test my gangster. Did they not know who the fuck I was? I was going to have to go to Fort. Lauderdale and body me a few niggas. Did they not know my body count was in double digits? I didn't think twice about digging a nigga their grave and putting their ass in it!

Lala was out with her friend shopping, so I sent her a quick text letting her know that I'd be home later on tonight. Lala had been kicking it with me at my crib for two weeks now. I was enjoying her company and getting to know her. I really liked the girl and my next move would be making us official.

It was nice having her in my arms at night and waking up to her beautiful face in the morning. I had it bad for the girl. It was to the point where I would go to the store and stock up on her feminine products. I studied her, and I was getting to know her inside and out.

Like how we had to sleep with the TV on because she was still scared of the dark. Or how she folded her cheese in little squares before she ate them. Before I took things further with her, I had to fly back up to Flint and have a talk with Donna. I was really thinking about bringing her with me so she could meet my grams.

Parking my car in front of one of the traps Bear told me he was holding the meeting at, I spotted him pistol-whipping a corner boy. Why the fuck would he do this shit outside of where my fucking drugs and money was? Did he not know that he was bringing unnecessary attention to my spot! I had to have a talk with that nigga for real because he was on some worst behavior type shit.

"Enough!" I said as I approached them. A few of the other corner put their hands up to their forehead saluting me. For a quick second, I could see Bear throw me shade, but I brushed it off. "What the fuck you doing, Bear?" I asked getting in his face.

"Man this was one of the young niggas that was supposed to be watching the spot. Ask him what he was doing when the trap got hit." I looked at the young dude, he didn't look no older than 18.

"What was you doing when them niggas came and got me for my drugs and money?" I asked, looking him in the face.

"I-I-I- made a quick stop to my girl's house," he stuttered.

"You did what nigga? You was in some pussy when you was suppose to be looking after my fucking money," I yelled, getting in his face. If looks could kill he would have been dead. "Ride with me," I said. He walked with me to the Honda I used to make my trips.

The whole drive to my little spot was quiet. I had this ducked off location that I used for reasons like this. Once we got to our destination, I got out the car and discreetly pulled out my fie.

PEW. PEW. PEW. The silencer put that nigga to rest for being so damn stupid. I hoped that pussy he was in was worth dying for because he'd just lost his life because of it. I went into my trunk and poured the gasoline all in the car before setting it on fire.

I took off my gloves and walked to the Toyota I had on stand by. I put my gun in the belly of a plush dog, and placed the dog in the 'I Love You' gift bag. I sat watching the car completely burn before I took off.

"How soon can you get to Fort Lauderdale?" I asked my brother Paco over the phone. I needed him to hang with Bear and watch over my business. I wasn't too confident in Bear and how he was running things.

"I'll be there in the morning bro," he answered. I really wanted both of my brothers to come down, but Pablo was in Columbia with Pops helping him with The Cartel.

"Good looking out bro." I really appreciated my brother coming down to help me.

"No problem bro, eso es lo que la familia es para. *(That's what family is for)*" As soon as we hung up, I made my way back to the trap to hold a very important meeting.

"This shit that happened today will not happen again," I said looking at all the men that sat at the table in their eyes. "Our purpose is to make money, not to lose it. Keep fucking with my money and I'mma start fucking with you lives!" I spoke with authority in my voice. I had to make sure these niggas was hearing me. I meant business! "I better not be short a penny next pick up. To ensure that we're on the same level my brother Paco will be down here in the morning to help Bear," I said looking at him. The look on his face was priceless.

"To look over me Stacks? Are you for real right now?" he asked, looking around for a camera as if his ass was on Punked and Ashton Kutcher was about to jump out on his ass.

"As serious as a heart attack. You of all people should know I don't play when it comes to my money. This is not up for discussion; my mind is made up. Paco will be here in the morning." I adjourned the meeting and made my way home.

When I walked in the house, I heard music blasting from the kitchen. I stood in doorway and watched Lala cook and dance to New Edition's *Cool It Now*. Her back was turned against me as she stirred something in a pot and moved her hips to the beat of the song. That ass was moving in those boy shorts and had rising Jr. from the dead. *All I keep thinking about is her in my arms, got to see what love is all about, and I'll never be the same until you are mine.* The words of the song played in my head. Yeah I had to make sure she was mine.

"How long you've been standing there?" she asked, snapping me out of my thoughts.

"Long enough," I replied, pulling her into my arms so we could dance to the rest of the song. I sang the lyrics in her ears meaning every word that came out of my mouth. She responded by sticking her tongue in my mouth and I welcomed it. I lifted her and sat her on the counter. I laid her down and pulled her shorts down. Ms. Pretty Pussy was the first thing that came to mind as I looked at her beautifully shaved vagina. I spread those lips apart and entered her world with my tongue.

"Ooooh my gooosh!" she moaned when I plunged my tongue deep in her. I never tasted anything so sweet in my life. It was as if she bathed in honey and sugar.

"Que el sabor tan bueno. *(That taste so good),*" I said before I dove back in, no life jacket. I made love to her pussy with my mouth, using my nose to stimulate her clit.

"Oh, I'm about to cum, oh, shit Stacks! Oh, gawd!" she pulled my head closer in her wetness threatening to drown me. I was just praying that she knew CPR. Her legs started shaking, and then I felt her body go limp. I licked and sucked her dry

"What's for dinner?" I asked, slipping her shorts back on her.

"You still hungry?" she seductively asked while biting on her bottom lip. She pulled me closer between her legs.

"You sure you're ready for this?" I asked as she led me up to the bedroom. She didn't answer me; all she did was undress, lay on the bed, and started playing in her pussy. I could see the wetness pour out of her and onto the sheets. I undressed and got in bed with her. I positioned myself between her legs and started sucking on her neck. Marking my territory, I made sure to leave multiple, visible hickies and bite marks on her. "Once you let me in, that's it. You're mine, the pussy is mine and any thoughts you have of James is dead. You heard?" I had to make sure this was really what she wanted because once I got in that pussy there was no way I was letting her ass go back to James.

She answered me by putting my dick in her slippery, wet mound. Her pussy suffocated my dick with its tightness. The stickiness of her moistness dripped on me with every thrust I took. I put one of her legs on my shoulders and used the curve in my dick to find that spot. *BINGO;* I thought as she moaned out.

"Oh shit, my spot." Now that I found it, there was no way I was going to stop hitting it. I had to make sure her spot and my dick became well acquainted because they were about to become lifelong friends. After hitting her spots a few more times, I felt her raining down on me. I pulled my dick out and went down to drink the everlasting water from her well.

Once she discharged that nut, she was selfishly holding back. I flipped her over and entered her from the back. I reached under her and played with her clit as the curve in my dick went to go greet her spot again.

"Ooooh, gawd this is not fair," she moaned.

"What's not fair," I asked teasing her.

"I'm about to c-c-c-cummm! Oh, no!!!" she came and collapsed on her stomach. She was in for a rude awakening if she thought I was done with her.

I rolled over with her on top of me and boy did she flip the script on me. Somehow she regained her composure and was riding me like I was one of those mechanical bulls and she was determined to stay on. She clasped her pussy around my dick and bounced up and down on it.

"Slow down ma!" I whispered, trying my hardest not to moan. But when she tightened her muscles again around my dick, I was singing another tune. "Ride this dick," I groaned, cheering her on. She was putting in work on my pole. She lifted all the way up and slid down on my dick and that was all it took for me to release my seeds in her.

She turned around with her back facing me and stuck my semi hard dick in her mouth. She started bouncing her ass cheeks as she deep throated my dick. She had all 10 inches of me down her throat and she ain't gag not once. Using her throat, she tried to swallow my dick. Not wanting to disrespect her by busting in her mouth, I flipped her over and went back to work.

"I'mma show you what this pussy could do," I said before making her cum back to back. We went at it for hours, round after round and not once did her pussy go dry on me. "You know you my girl now?" I asked as she laid in my arms exhausted from the fuck-a-thon we just had.

"Yes, baby I know," was her last words before she drifted off to sleep. *Lord if this is your will please make it work*; I silently prayed before I pulled her close to me and closed my eyes.

"Breakfast is ready!" Lala's beautiful voice woke me up by sitting the breakfast tray over me.

"Thanks Ma'," I said looking down at the cheese eggs, steak, toasted bagels, fresh fruits, and a tall glass of some type of smoothie drink. My stomach instantly jumped for joy anticipating the taste of the food that the aroma had my nose in pure bliss.

I got up, brushed my teeth, and went in. I was on a mission to demolish this plate of food. After eating, I went downstairs to find Lala. The kitchen was cleaned, but she wasn't in there. Hearing the sound of the shower, I went inside the bathroom. The smell of strawberries bum-rushed me as soon as I opened the door. I quickly undressed and joined her in the shower for a rematch.

"So, are you going to tell me about Donna?" Lala asked sitting on the edge of the bed while applying lotion to her body.

"Are you going to tell me about James?" I shot at her while pulling a shirt over my head and grabbing the aromatherapy oil off the dresser.

"What do you want to know?" She looked at me as I grabbed one of her feet.

"Everything." I poured the oil in the palm of my hands and began massaging her foot.

"Well we met when I was 15. He was so ugly," she said chuckling. "No girls would give him the time of day, so he stopped trying to talk to girls period. I was attracted to his personality; he was funny, silly, and adventurous. There was a never a dull moment with him. Well, after his dad left they started to struggle. They lost their house and had to move to the projects.

Even though my parents didn't approve of him anymore because he wasn't in the academy or living in the suburbs, I still went behind their backs to visit him. Their living arrangements was horrible. Their housemaid, Betty the roach was the first thing that greeted me as soon as I walked through the door. I could tell that he was embarrassed.

That's when he came up with the bright idea to start selling drugs. Around that time, my parents cut me off financially because my grades started to slip and I was out hanging with 'hoodlums' as they would say. My dad came up with a bright idea that I get a job. He had a friend that owned a few Burger Kings so he got me a job there to prove a point.

I could still remember his words 'If you continue with the nonsense Lala this is the type of job you'll work for the rest of your life.' Anywho, with my paychecks, I gave them to James to help finance his dream of being a street pharmacist. When my parents found out my boyfriend were a drug dealer, they blew a casket. My father was a celebrity surgeon and he didn't want me to ruin his career he worked so hard for and my mother being so weak minded she followed him."

Lala took a deep breath and I could tell that she was hurt behind her parents' actions. "So Lisa and I got a job at KOD. Her, James, and I moved into a two-bedroom apartment and while we stripped, he sold drugs. Instead of going off to college like I was suppose to do, I was at the club shaking my ass. When James finally got his business up and running, I quit the club and went back to school. With money comes hoes and that's when we started having problems. He was so used to girls not liking him that when a few started to look his way, he decided to makeup for all the lost time." She started to cry so I held her.

"Growing up, it was just my mother and I. I had the best of everything, but I did not have a father. Every time I would ask my mother about my father she would shake it off and try to 'buy' her way out of answering me. When my mother died when I was 17, she left me a letter about my father. Enclosed in the envelope were a few pictures of him and his address.

I flew to Columbia with every intention of killing him, but when he presented me with an offer of making millions, I decided why not, I had nothing to lose. He made sure I finished school and went to college. I also had a little band that used to perform at the local Jazz bar for fun. Then I met her. Donna was the first girl I fell in love with," I spoke.

"I too was guilty of putting a woman that loved you more than life itself through hell. The day she caught me cheating on her was the day I vowed it would be the last time I do her wrong. She was pregnant with my twins and she deserved better. I was going to make her my wife. I had enough money to leave the game, we were going to move down to Columbia, get married, and start our family," I paused, pondering if I wanted to relive the worst day in my life. "She was taken from me."

Lala held me as the tears started to fall from my eyes.

"I came home one day and she was dead. The motherfuckers tortured her until she gave them access to a room that had all my drugs and money. Then they shot her in the stomach three times and slit her throat." I sobbed uncontrollably thinking how she couldn't even have an open casket funeral. I cried for my twins that never got a chance to make it into this world. I cried for my mother who wasn't here now to see that I found a woman to finally help fill this void. My mind started playing tricks on me because I swear I heard Donna telling me that it was ok to move on and be happy.

Chapter 15

James

When it rains it pours, I thought as I puffed on this Rainbow Kush I bought from one of the local corner boys. This shit was some fie shit. Ever since Lala left me, I didn't feel the same. My money was drying up and the one person who would have made this all better was gone. You never really knew what you have until it was gone. I wished I treated her better. Sex ain't better than love because the hoes that I was getting sex from no longer wanted to deal with me because I wasn't the big man on the streets. I knew Lala would have stuck it out with a nigga. She was riding when a nigga ain't even have a pot to piss in or a window to throw it out of.

I had to get my baby back. It'd been three months too long without her and playtime was over. I needed my wife here with me where she belonged. I called her for the 20th time today and got the voicemail again. She could dead all thoughts of her and Stacks living happily ever after because I soon as I caught up to that nigga, I was pushing his wig back.

"Oh, shit," Ashley yelled, jumping out her sleep and running to the bathroom. I swear all she did was throw the fuck up. I was too ready for this pregnancy to be over, so that she could free my youngin'. Even though, I'd been kicking it with her since Lala been gone, she wasn't wifey material. I didn't know why I fucked around and got that hoe pregnant. "This baby don't agree with nothing I eat," she whined while walking out of the bathroom and getting back in bed.

I got out of bed to get ready for my day. This hoe had life all types of fucked up if she thought we was about to lay up in bed like we was the Brady bunch or some shit.

"Where you going?" she asked, noticing me getting dressed.

"Out," I replied walking out the door. I had to get up with Rico and see what our next move was going to be. He told me that some jack boys in Fort Lauderdale had some weight they wanted to sell; hell anything was better than nothing. I was ready to get back in the game by any means.

"Yo, what the lick read?" Rico answered the phone.

"Shit that's why I'm calling you. What's up with UPS, did they come through with the package?" I spoke in codes.

"Nah, they left a notice on the door for us to come pick it up," he replied playing along.

"No doubt, I'll be on yo' side in a few," I said hanging up and parking my car. First thing first I had to make things right with wifey.

***

I walked into the entrance of Jackson Memorial Hospital. If she wasn't going to talk to me over the phone then she had no choice but to talk to me face to face.

"Hey, is Lala here?" I asked one of her co-workers that was sitting at the nurse's station.

"She went to the cafeteria to study," a nurse passing by replied as she pushed a lady in a wheelchair.

"Thanks." I made my way to the elevator and with every floor I passed, the more my heart rate sped up. I felt so nervous, like I was about to ask her on a date for the first time or some shit. Entering the cafeteria, I spotted her in the far corner sitting on an auburn colored sofa. She looked so cute with her glasses on and a serious look on her face as she stared into a book.

She was chewing on the end of her pen, a bad habit she had while she was studying. I kicked myself for pushing the love of my life into the arms of another man.

"Is this seat taken?" I walked over to her and sat down.

"What do you want, James?" she snapped.

"I just wanted to talk," I pleaded, hoping like hell she was going to hear me out.

"Ok, talk," she said with her eyes still plastered in the book that was in her lap.

"I did a lot of fucked up things in our relationship and I'm sorry. I wasn't ready yet to be a man. It took me losing everything to realize that all I ever wanted in a wife was right in front of me." I got on bended knee and took her hand. "Lala, I know I fucked up, but no man is perfect. If you would have me, I would love to make things right. I want to make you my wife." I pulled out the little black box I had in my back pocket and opened it. I used my thumb to wipe the tears away from her eyes as I slid the ring on her finger.

"You think it's that fucking easy, James?! You think you can come in here with a weak ass apology and a ring to make things better. It took you eight fucking years to put this ring on my damn finger, James! It took my being with another man to finally make you realize you had something good!" she yelled, taking the ring off her finger and throwing it. "Go give this ring to that bitch Keyshia because I don't want it," she yelled in my face.

"Answer me this, what did your results say when you went to the clinic?" I asked, knowing damn well this 'Keyshia' shit was a lie! She just sat there and looked at me. We both knew that it came back negative, Well at least I knew for a fact that mine did. "Ok then, just hear me out. Let me take you to dinner, so we can talk." I asked, praying she would give me another chance.

"Ok," she simply said before gathering her things and walking out. Something was better than nothing at this point.

***

"How much you selling each brick?" I asked this nigga named Nano who claimed he had some good shit.

"I got 12 and I'll let them off for 17 if you buy all of them." Each brick was going for 17,500 so to get twelve at 17 wasn't that bad. Nico and I both went half on it. I only had 200,000 left to my name and I just spent 105,000 of that on drugs. After purchasing the bricks, I felt a little better. If we flipped it right then the money would be enough for me to get my shit together until I could find a legit connect instead of a jack boy.

As soon as we made it back to Miami, I called my team and told them it was time to get back to work. For the first time in a while, I found myself smiling, I had one more chance to get it right with Lala and I was about to get my money right. I wanted Stacks to feel what I felt when he took everything away from me before I ended his life. I hope he enjoyed the taste of my girl's pussy because that would be his last supper.

Chapter 16

Bear

"Did he buy them from you?" I asked Nano over the phone. He had a meeting with that nigga James to buy the bricks I stole from my own trap. If things went as planned, then a war was about to break out between Stacks and James.

"Yeah, I only sold that nigga half, so he could come back and re-up"

"Good looking out bra, tight work," I said licking my blunt and sealing it close. I spoke and chopped it up some more with Nano over the phone so that we could discuss more of my plan before hanging up the phone. I had to pick up Lisa because we had plans on going bowling. A nigga wasn't the bowling type, but hey I had to do what I had to do. Taking Stacks down was so serious to me that I had to do whatever it took to ensure that he was dead and gone.

"Out with that bitch for the eighth time this week," Tasha said, walking in on the ending of the conversation I just had with Lisa.

"Man I ain't with that shit today for real," I said and fired up another blunt. Dog was known to be a man's best friend, but weed was mine. I was what they called a certified weed head. I couldn't last a day without smoking a minimum amount of five blunts a day

"You never take me out as much as you take the bitch out," she said putting her hands on her hips.

"What you want me to take your ass out and risk Stacks seeing you?"

"Stacks is in Miami nigga, we about a two hour drive away from his ass!" she yelled trying get saucy with a nigga

"You dumb for real though, I'm out woe." I got up and left. I ain't have to have this bitch in my ear hollering about irrelevant shit. At the end of the day, she was the bitch I planned on moving to the private island with, but if she kept with the fuck shit; Lisa could easily replace her.

***

"STRIKE!" Lisa yelled, jumping up and down as she hit all the bowling ball pins. "Who's coming for me?" she started twerking doing her victory dance. I wasn't complaining watching that ass bounce.

"I bet you can't beat me shooting dice though." I grabbed her by her waist. I knew I had a purpose for being with her, but a nigga was starting to feel her.

"Stop being a sore loser." She turned around and kissed me on the lips.

"You ready to go eat?" I asked, trying to get out of that lovey dovey kissing shit.

"Yeah, oooh you have to try this spot called Fingalicking on 32nd they have the best macaroni in the world," she said.

"Lead the way then," I told her as I tossed her my car keys. Yeah a nigga had this bitch pushing his whip, while I sat back a rolled daddies.

"Welcome to Fingalicking! Dine-In or takeout?" the sexy ass waitress asked us. If I wasn't with Lisa, I would have been trying get up in them jeans that hugged that ass to perfection.

"Dine-In," Lisa said noticing me checking ol'girl out.

"Follow me," Ms. thickness said as she brought us to our seat.

"That ass fat though," Lisa joked, noticing me watching the way the waitress' ass jiggled.

"Huh?" I said confused.

"I saw that ass too, it was sitting up nice in them jeans," she laughed. I was glad she wasn't on no jealous type of shit. If it was Tasha's ass then I would have been all types of 'fuck niggas'.

"Are you ready to order?" Ms. Thickness asked when she came back. She tapped her pencil against the notepad she held in her hand.

"I'll have the fried chicken dinner with seafood rice, collard greens, and extra mac and cheese," Lisa ordered without even picking up the menu.

"And for you sir?"

"I'll have the fried cat fish dinner with extra mac and cheese, green beans with two extra slices of cornbread," I said, handing her my menu. After scribbling down the orders, she walked off, but not before she discreetly gave me a wink. Yeah the bitches were feeling a chubby nigga and if you ain't got you one you better get in. Skinny niggas wasn't in style no more.

Midway through our meal, Lisa excused herself to the restroom. I flagged the waitress down, took down her number, and ordered me a to go plate for later on. *Damn this mac is good;* I thought as I first degree murdered the plate.

"You on a date and still getting numbers." I looked up and saw Stacks' ass looking at me. Bitch ass nigga.

"You know how it is," I replied trying my hardest to hide all the hate I had for the nigga.

"Was that Lala's home girl you was with?" he asked me with a serious look on his face.

"Yeah, Lisa. Why?" I asked hoping this nigga wasn't about to tell me he was smashing her.

"Just asking," he said with a look of confusion on his face. "Well, I'm out, enjoy your date. Be easy," he said before he picked up his food at the counter and walked of. Pussy ass nigga had my trigger finger itching.

Lisa came back to the table and we finished up our food and made small talk. Talking to her, our conversation was always on a different level. We spoke about stuff that made me think. If I could figure out a way to follow through with my plan and keep her on my team, I'd kick Tasha's worn out pussy ass to the side in a heartbeat. That bitch wasn't nothing but a headache anyways.

"You coming back to my house?" Lisa asked with sex on her mind. I knew she couldn't get enough of this dick. Name a big nigga that had a 9 ½ inch dick that knew how to do overtime in that pussy without getting tired.

"For sho," I answered, finishing that last crumb on my plate before washing it down with a glass of homemade peach sweet tea. This place right here was the truth for real.

Pulling out the money to cover our meal and a few extra hundreds to tip the waitress, we made our way out hand in hand. A nigga was on full and ready to put in work tonight. I planned on sleeping in that pussy tonight. *Fuck Tasha*; I thought as I turned my phone completely off.

Chapter 17

Ashley

I couldn't believe this nigga was still fucking with Lala's bitch ass and I was the one carrying his first child! I was pissed as fuck sitting here watching them look like the world's greatest couple. What really ticked me off was when they got in his car.

I allowed them to get down the street before I followed them back to his house. I wanted to get out the car and snatch her ass up, but I played it cool, her end was near soon. I watched them walk into the house. What killed me was that the hoe had been shacked up with the next nigga for a little over three months, but now she wanted to get back in my nigga's face like damn hoe how much dicks can your pussy take? I knew she was an undercover thot, I wasn't buying that "Oh she's loyal" bullshit.

"Arrrgh." I opened the car door and allowed everything I ate for dinner paint the floor. I was sick of this little bastard in me. I didn't know what the fuck was taking Bear and Ted so long to carry out their plan. I was ready for them to get rid of Lala so that I could kill this little piece of shit in me before it was too late. I just needed the baby to make sure James stuck around.

After they killed Lala's ass, he would have no choice but to stay with me. Scrolling through my phone, I found Ted's number and called him.

"What's good fam?" he answered.

"What the fuck is taking so long getting rid of Lala's ass?! I'm sick of seeing that bitch in my nigga's face," I snapped getting right to the point. I ain't have no time for small talk.

"Just chill cuz, everything take a little time, but we on that," he replied, trying to calm me down.

"Hurry the fuck up before I get out this car and kill that bitch myself. She up there in my man's house probably sucking his dick and shit!" The thought of Lala and James fucking had me 38 hot!

"He with her now?" he asked with a hint of excitement in his voice.

"Yes I watched them walked inside. I'm out here parked in front of the house now," I replied taking a swig of my water hoping like hell this baby was not about to have me throwing up again. I swear this little devil in me was evil as hell.

"When they come out snap some pictures of them then send it to me."

"Do I look like a fucking private investigator?" I snapped on his dumb ass for asking me to do some shit like that.

"Man just do it, trust me this will make things go way faster," he reasoned with me.

"How?" I asked wanting to know what the hell me taking pictures of Lala and James was going to do to speed up the process.

"Man just do it!" he said getting annoyed and hanging up.

When they finally came out of the house, it was 11pm. They was all hugged up and fucking for three damn hours. I snapped as many pictures as I could before they got in the car and pulled off. Something had to give because this bitch was fucking shit up for me.

***

Pulling in my driveway, I noticed James' car wasn't there. I called him three times back to back only for him to forward my calls. Oh, he wanted to play? Well, I was good with the games. I was even a good magician because I had a trick for his ass. I went in the house and sat on the couch. I scrolled down my phone and sent him a text.

I sat back with my legs crossed and waited for him to call and just like clock work my phone started ringing. I let the first call go to the voicemail before I finally answered.

"Hello?" I faintly answered the phone.

"What's good ma, the baby ok?" he asked sounding so concerned for the little demon.

"Oh, my God baby, it hurts so bad," I dramatically cried into the phone as if I was really in pain.

"What happened?" he worriedly asked.

"I got up and went to the bathroom and when I got up there was so much blood, I'm in so much pain. Oh, James I think I'm losing the baby," I cried harder.

"Don't move ma, I'm on my way," he said, hanging up the phone. I hung up the phone while laughing at his dumb ass.

Not long after, I heard the keys in the door and I quickly laid on the ground and closed my eyes.

"Yo Ash, where you at ma'?" I heard him yelling for me. "C'mon ma get up," he said picking me up.

"It hurts so bad," I whispered as I cried in his neck, hiding the fact that I was actually cracking the fuck up.

"Ok, I'mma get you to a hospital," he said carrying me to the car. He laid me in the backseat and sped off running every red light and stop sign.

***

"Can I get a nurse please?" James asked walking over to the nurse's station with me cradled in his arms.

This shit was so comical, it reminded me of the movie Menace to Society when Kane got shot and the rushed him in the E.R.

"Sir, what's wrong with her?" a nurse asked, rushing over to us.

"She's pregnant and she's been bleeding and having really bad cramps," James replied with a somber look on his face. That was what he got for playing with me, now I was about to play with his emotions

"Oh, God, I think I'm having a miscarriage," I cried holding my stomach as if I was really in pain.

"Can you help her please!" James sounded as if he was about to cry, poor baby. The icing on the cake was when the nurse told him that he had to sit in the waiting room while I got examined. Good, now he could sit out there with his thoughts driving him crazy wondering if his first child was going to make it or not. Ha! Teach him to play with me.

Three pokes in my arm and a urine sample later, I was laying in the hospital bed waiting on my results.

"Is everything ok with the baby?" James asked as he walked into the room and took a seat next to my bed.

"I don't know, I hope so," I lied. To be honest, I could really careless.

"Ms. Perkins, I'm nurse Glenda and I'm going to perform an ultrasound so that we can check on the baby." She squeezed this cold ass gel on my stomach and began looking for the baby. Once she found it, for a brief moment my heart skipped a beat. Looking at my baby on the screen, I actually considered keeping it; however, under the circumstances that I conceived the baby, I quickly dismissed the thought.

I looked over at James who had his face glued to the little screen with a smile on his face. For the first time, I felt a little bad about him never getting to meet the baby that he thought was his.

"Ok, well I'm done here. The doctor will be in here shortly to speak with you. Feel better Ms. Perkins," the nurse spoke before she left.

Years later, the doctor decided to show his face. I was about to get real ignorant with his ass too. I was hungry, tired, and this hospital was giving me the damn creeps.

"Ms. Perkins, everything looks fine. The baby is ok with a nice strong heartbeat. I am going to put you on bed rest for two weeks. So, for two weeks no work, sex, or lifting anything. The only thing you need to get out of bed to do is go to the restroom. Do you have anyone at home that can help you?" he asked me while scribbling something down in my chart.

"I'll help her, Doc," James spoke up. The thought of him being home with me for two whole weeks had me doing the happy dance.

"Good. This is a prescription for your Prenatal Vitamins. I also want you to follow up with your doctor in two weeks. If you do not have a doctor, here is a list of some," he said handing me a folder. "Oh, and before I forget, here are the pictures of your baby." He handed me an envelope that James took from me. The doctor also handed me some discharge paper to sign then he said his goodbyes. I quickly got dressed and we left the hospital

On the drive home, James kept talking me to death on how happy he was to finally become a father. I didn't want to rain on his parade by telling him that he would never father this baby in me, so I let him carry on. I wish I had some headphones because he was becoming so annoying.

It was baby this and baby that, like damn shut the fuck up. I wanted to scream and tell him that the baby wasn't even his, but that would only ruin the plans. I didn't even really care for the paternity of my child because that was a bridge I didn't plan on having to cross.

As long as everything went according to plan and quick, everything was good. I faked sleep just so he could take the hint and shut up. I wasn't mad that he was excited about the baby, I was more mad at the nurse for showing me the baby and having me feel some type of way. Either way, it was getting sucked out of me, I couldn't keep it even if I wanted to.

Chapter 18

Stacks

Life with Lala was great. She showed me how it felt to be in love with her all over again. She was everything a man could dream of. She was smart, sexy, and a freak. Plus she had wife qualities; she could cook, kept the house clean, and was always there asking how a nigga day was. I was on cloud nine with my boo.

"Are you listening to me?" Lala asked me as she stood in front of me in this short ass black, tight dress. I paid attention to her stomach; I knew she was pregnant. My grandma called me the other day saying she was dreaming of fishes, and that she saw a baby lizard in her room. I also knew she hadn't had a period. One thing about me was that, I played real close attention to my woman. I knew her like clockwork.

"No, put it back," I told her bringing my attention to that little ass dress she wanted to buy.

"Why bae?" she whined, giving me the puppy dog sad face.

"Because I don't want to have to go to jail for murder, now put it back!" The way these Miami niggas was thirsty I knew without a doubt they would try to step on my toes at any given moment.

"I'm hungry," Lala said as we walked out of the mall hand and hand.

"What you want to eat?" I asked as I opened the car door for her.

"Can you make me burgers and fried?" She put on her seatbelt and began munching on a big bag of sunflower seeds. This was another reason how I knew she was pregnant; she had a newfound love for them things. I wasn't going to press the issue though. She probably didn't know and if she did, I'd let her tell me on her own.

As soon as we got home, I got in the kitchen to make dinner. While I was flipping the burgers, Lala came in the kitchen and grabbed a big bag of Cool Ranch Doritos and started eating them.

"The food almost done," I said, eyeing her suspiciously. Lately she'd been eating a lot more, too.

"Ok bae, can you make my burger a double with cheese and bacon?" she asked while licking the crumbs off her fingers.

"Yes ma'am," I replied while shaking my head. I wanted to go out and buy her a damn test, but I'd let her do that on her own.

Once dinner was done, we sat at the table and ate. "How would you feel about going to Flint with me to meet my grams?" I asked her before taking a sip of my soda. She took two big bites of her burger.

"I would love to meet her," she finally answered, diving right back into her food. I decided to let her pig out and save this conversation for another day. Two double cheeseburgers and fries later, Lala finally decided she had enough and helped me clear the table. We cleaned up the kitchen and went upstairs to prepare for bed.

I heard the shower and decided to join her. Right when I was about to make my way in the bathroom, a calendar caught my attention. I flipped through the pages and noticed that with every month there was a red circle around a day except for last month.

Yeah she's pregnant; I thought as I picked up a pen and wrote **GO GET A TEST!** The thought of having another baby scared me, but I was happy at the same time. I didn't want to get too high only to be disappointed if she wasn't really pregnant, but something deep down inside told me she was.

I got in the shower behind her and started kissing on her neck. "Mmmmm," she moaned as she threw her head back. I gently lifted one of her legs and entered her. "Oh shiiiit Stacks," she sang as I started digging in them guts.

I lifted her out of the shower and laid her on the marble countertop, placing her legs on my shoulders.

"Bae slow down," she said, throwing me off. Usually, Lala loved for a nigga to go knee deep in her, so for her to tell me to slow down puzzled me. "It hurts." She placed her hands on my abs slowing down my thrust.

"Lala you pregnant?" I asked wanting to know why all of a sudden she couldn't take the dick. She looked at me as if I just told her I was gay or some shit.

"No, why y-you ask?" she stuttered.

"You eating like you been starving, now all of a sudden I'm going too deep for you, makes me think that cervix door is shut closed," I said slowly sliding in and out of her.

"Noooo, bae I'm not pregnant," she said moaning as I took my dick out and used it to tease her clit.

"You sure?" I asked sliding deep in her again.

"Yes bae, now shut up and fuck me," and with that I made love to her. We got in the shower, washed off, and got ready to go to bed.

While in bed, Lala and I was watching re-runs of Martin when my phone started to ring. I looked at my phone as saw it was Bear calling me, so I decided to let him talk to my voicemail. Five minutes later, my phone started to beep. I looked down at the text and saw it was a message from Bear with our 911 code, so I decided to call him back.

"Yo' fam, you need to come meet up with ASAP," Bear greeted me.

"Why what's good, everything a'ight?" I asked praying that none of my traps got touched.

"Yo' kid it's about ya girl," he said.

"What about her?" I asked walking out of the room so Lala wouldn't be all in my mouth.

"Word is she was out with ol' boy the other day." Once he said that, I felt the wind get knocked out of my body.

"How you know?" I asked, not wanting to jump to conclusion.

"Ted was fucking with a bitch around the way from where ol' boy stay and he spotted her coming out of his house, he even snapped a few pics for you," Bear said making me mad all over again. I wanted to go and snap Lala's neck, but I had to see the proof first.

"A'ight I be on that side in a little bit, holla at Ted for me," I said, hanging up the phone. I counted to ten in my head slowly before I went back in the room and got dressed.

"Where you going?" she asked as soon as she noticed that I was putting my clothes on and getting ready to leave.

"Out to handle business, go to sleep and I'll be back in a few," I said walking out the room. I had to get out of there fast. There was no telling what I would do to Lala if I stayed in that house with her ass.

I jumped in my hooptie and made that drive to the Dale. I was hoping like hell Lala wasn't fucking with that nigga after I told her that once I got up in her it was a wrap for them. I was so mad that I didn't even notice the police behind me until the flashing blue and white lights brought me back to reality. Damn!

Chapter 19

Lala

It felt weird lying in Stacks' bed without him. He was usually home by 12 a.m. the latest and it was now 4 a.m. and still no sign of him. I'd been calling him back to back and all I got was the voicemail. I hoped like hell he wasn't cheating on me. I knew he was too good to be true.

I snuggled up with his pillow and went to check all my social network accounts. The sound of the door closing brought a smile on my face. Daddy was home; I missed my baby all day. I could hear him coming up the stairs. Although my back was towards the door, I could feel his presence in the doorway.

"Where did you go the other day when you left and didn't come home until 11?" he asked sitting on the edge of the bed. I could smell the weed and liquor on his breath.

"Out to eat with Lisa," I lied to him. I went out to eat, but it wasn't with Lisa. James begged me to hear him out and I did. We reminisced and had a great time. Laying on the bed as he ate me out, made me realize that I was finally over him. When my body didn't react to him the way it usually did, I knew it was a wrap for us.

I was falling in love with Stacks and he was who I decided I was going to be with. But the question was why was Stacks questioning me about shit that happened days ago?

"I'm going to ask you this one more time and Lala it will be in your best interest not to lie to me. Where were you that day!?" He rose off the bed and looked at me. My heart rate started to speed up. Did he know? No. He couldn't have known. If he did then why didn't he bring it up that day? So I stuck with my story.

"I was with Lisa," I answered him.

"Where did you and Lisa go?" he asked, his back was still towards me so I was not able to read his facial expression.

"We went to Applebee's then back to her house to have a little girl talk." I was surprised how fast that lie rolled off my tongue. Stacks started to laugh, which confused the hell out of me.

"What you're not about to do is lie to me," Stacks said getting off the bed and walking to the closet. I sat up in the bed and watched him pack his clothes.

My heart felt so heavy. I couldn't believe this shit. I wanted to cry, but I didn't want to look guilty, even though I was.

"It's funny how you was with Lisa, when Lisa was with Bear that day," he said. My heart sank down to the pit of my stomach. I was at lost for words. He packed more of his things while mumbling in Spanish. "After all that nigga did to you, you decided to go back!! I showed you how it felt to be treated like a queen. I shared with you personal details of my life that I never talk about. I told you once you allowed me between your legs that you were mine and you go back to the nigga that broke you after it took me so long to rebuild you. That same nigga that had you second guessing yourself. That has a bitch carrying his baby, but that's what you want. You like to be treated like shit. I'm sorry I was too much of a man for you, Lala," he said while stuffing more of his things into his luggage.

"It's not even like that," I cried.

"Then what is it like? Please tell me because I am lost." He finally turned towards me and looked at me. I wish he hadn't because the look he was giving me broke my heart. "It was just dinner, he needed closure," I said praying for God to save me from this dilemma I was in.

"Closure Lala? Why did you lie? Why couldn't you keep it real with me? Most importantly, how the fuck did you end up at the nigga's house?" He came closer to me and grabbed me by the neck. "Did you fuck him!?" he yelled in my face. I'd never seen him so angry in my life. I shook my head no and he let me go.

"I don't have nothing else to say to you since you want to lie," he said, picking up his bags and walking out the room.

"I'm not lying," I said running after him. "I'm sorry for lying, I'm sorry for having dinner with him without telling you, but we did not have sex," I pleaded with him.

"So what did y'all do?" he asked turning around facing me. I chewed on my bottom lip contemplating on whether I should be honest or not.

"We went to his house to talk, one thing led to another, and we ummm well he uhhh," I stuttered on my words not sure on how I was going to complete my sentence.

"He did what, Lala?!" Stacks said raising his voice.

"H-h-he umm he kinda of sorta gave me oral sex."

WHAM!

Stacks backhanded me. I could feel my lip swell up. I wasn't mad that he hit me, I was more mad at myself for fucking up something good.

"You can stay here as long as you want to, I'm out. I really did love you, Lala, but you played me real good." He picked up his luggage and walked out the door. I ran behind him not wanting something so good end. For the first time in forever, I was happy. I had a man that loved and cared about me. I had everything that I couldn't get from James in Stacks, but I messed it all up.

"Please baby, don't go. I love you Anthony, please don't leave me. I am so sorry, it will never happen again. I swear. Please don't leave me please?" I threw my arms over him and cried. The fact that he didn't hug me back or try to console me let me know it was a lost cause.

"Go in the house Lala, you're half naked." The fact that I was standing outside in my bra and panties didn't bother me. My main concern was making sure he did not get in that car and leave.

He picked me up and carried me inside and over to the couch. He gently put me down and left. All I could do was sit there and cry. It was all my fault I was so stupid. I cried so much I ended up throwing up everything I'd eaten for dinner. Instead of getting up, I cried myself to sleep right there on the bathroom floor.

***

I thought I was going to wake up to breakfast, flowers, or even some sweet kisses. Boy was I wrong. The only thing I woke up to was a horrible headache. I got up and walked over to the sink to brush my teeth. I looked in the mirror and noticed my red, swollen puffy eyes and my oversized lip.

I called off from work and got in bed. I laid on Stacks' side of the bed remembering all the great memories we had in this bed. *He is such a sweetheart*; I thought as I picked up the phone and called the only person that I knew that would come to my rescue.

"Hello," Lisa answered, sounding half asleep.

"He left me," I cried into the phone letting it all out.

"Text me the address. I'm on my way," she said sounding like she was ready to put on her cape and fly over here. Stacks didn't really like people knowing where he lived, but since he moved out I didn't see the issue. I sent Lisa a text with Stacks' address.

After a while, I went to unlock the door for her and laid back in bed. I cried until I had no more tears left to cry then I just laid there looking at the wall.

"What happened?" Lisa asked, getting in bed with me.

"He found out. How could I be so stupid?" I responded, giving her a somber look.

"Lala, I told you this was a bad idea. You should have just left James alone in the past," she scolded me.

"I know and it's too late now because he's gone," I cried. All I wanted to do was to wake up in the arms of my man, but the chances of that happening were slim to none. I got up out of bed and ran to the bathroom again throwing up everything.

"Lala, are you pregnant?" Lisa asked, handing me a washcloth.

"Don't be silly, Lisa." First Stacks now her. What was up with people thinking I was pregnant? "I'm on the… oh, my God! No!!" I couldn't believe I was so careless. After I left James, I never refilled my birth control pills now there was a chance of me being pregnant by a guy that didn't want anything to do with me.

"You want to go grab breakfast and then pick up a test?" Lisa asked rubbing my back.

"No I just want to lay down, can you get one for me please?" I got up and picked up my calendar to see if in fact I was late. The tears started to pour down my face as I read Stacks' note. He knew all along. I got back in bed and tried my best to go to sleep.

An hour later, Lisa came into the room with a plate of food and a Walgreen's bag. I wasn't really hungry, so I grabbed the Walgreen's bag from her and went into the bathroom. I peed on the stick and put it on the counter. I decided to take a shower to kill time.

Before I could even fully lather my body, Lisa burst through the bathroom door and announced that she was going to be a Godmother. Well I'll be damned! Great, I was going to be a mother, and I was not married, hell I wasn't even in a relationship with my child's father. I finished my shower and got dressed.

"What are you going to do?" Lisa asked me while chumping on a piece of bacon.

"I'm keeping it," I said getting back in bed a pulling the covers over my head.

Lisa stayed over for majority of the day. After cleaning and ordering me some takeout, she left to go on her date with Bear. I was so happy that my bestie was finally settling down. At least if I wasn't going to have any happiness, she could. I considered calling Stacks, but decided to text him the news.

Me: *I know I'm the last person you want to talk to right now, but I have something really important to tell you.*

I sent it and held my breath waiting for a response

Bae: *what is it?*

Me: *I rather tell you face to face.*

Bae: *Bye Lala I don't have time for the games right now.*

Me: *I'm pregnant.* While waiting on his response, I drifted off to sleep.

***

I woke up to someone rubbing my stomach and I thought I was dreaming until I heard Stacks' voice.

"Is it mine?" he asked, looking me in the eyes.

"Yes," I whispered.

"You sure?" he rose his eyebrow at me like I was some fucking slut.

"Yes! But if you don't want to be in my child's life I understand." I played with my nails. I really needed a fill in, but that wasn't important at the moment.

"I'll take your word, that's my child and I'll always be there for him or her." I was relieved when he said that. Even if we weren't together, at least we could co-parent.

"How far along are you?" he asked.

"The test estimated 2-3 weeks."

"The test told you that?" he asked with a look of confusion on his face.

"Yes, I took one of those new Clear Blue Easy that estimates how far along you are," I told him.

"Well, when are you going to the doctor?" he asked while still rubbing on my stomach.

"I haven't set an appointment yet."

"Well, what are you waiting for?" he asked, pulling me in his arms. It felt so good to be in his arms again.

"When I feel better," I cried as he held me.

"Shhh, stop crying, you're going to stress my baby out. It's going to be ok," he tried to reassure me.

"Are you coming back home?" I asked hoping he would forgive me.

"No," he answered.

"Why?"

"Are you hungry?" he asked trying to change the subject.

"No, just leave," I said, giving up. I expected him to get up and walk out the door, but all he did was hold me tighter as I silently cried.

"I'm sorry, Anthony, I just want us to be a real family. Please forgive me," I begged.

"Go to sleep ma, we'll talk about this later."

Chapter 20

Bear

I finally got the information I needed by following Lisa. Lala called her early this morning telling her that Stacks left her. When she told me, she had to go over to Stacks' house to check up on her, I wanted to jump up and start doing the 2-step.

Instead, I acted disappointed that she was going to be leaving. I followed behind her keeping a safe distance between us and viola; I found where that nigga had been hiding. I never felt so happy in my life. To finally be able to take down the enemy was a great feeling.

Now that the ball was in my court, I decided to call a quick time out and plan this out. Stacks had become a hard a hard target to hit, so I had to plan this one out real good.

"Yo' nigga what's good?" I said giving Ted dap as soon as I pulled up to the spot.

"This nigga is starting to be a real big problem," he answered with a scowl on his face.

"What nigga?"

"Man Stacks' brother!" he yelled throwing his hands up.

"Who that nigga Paco?" I asked.

"Yeah man that nigga walking around here enforcing shit like he the damn law or some shit. He had the audacity to tell me how to run my blocks. The fuck this nigga got going on!?!" Ted yelled fuming.

"Oh, yeah? Well looks like we just have to handle that nigga then. No pressure," I said and sat down to roll a fattie.

"Was you able to get some information out of ol' girl?" Ted said putting more weed in a grinder to roll another blunt.

"You won't believe this shit nigga," I said, firing up the blunt.

"What?" he asked rolling up another blunt.

"She brought me to his house!" I passed the weed.

"Man, stop fucking with me?" He inhaled weed before passing it back to me.

"G-shit! I guess he left Lala or some shit like that. Well, Lisa went over there to console her, and brought me right in front of his front door!" I said unable to contain my excitement.

"Well, if that is the case, why we not over there busting a cap in that nigga's ass," Ted said, pulling out his gun and sitting it on his lap, ready for war. My nigga.

"I still don't know where he keeping the drugs and money."

"Serpientes merece morir. *(Snakes deserve to die),*" a voice behind us said scaring the fuck out of me. I jumped up and pulled out my gun pointing it at Paco.

"That's how you treat my brother after he has been nothing but good to you, pedazo de mierda *(piece of shit)?"* Paco said with one gun pointing in my direction and another on Ted.

"If you know what's good for you, you'd back down son, you out numbered," I said ready to pull the trigger.

"I will die for my blood if I have to, but just know if I die, I will not be dying alone," he said through gritted teeth. His voice bounced off the walls with power just like Stacks. The last part of his sentence 'I will not be dying alone' made me feel uneasy.

POW! POW! Paco shot Ted in the arm twice causing him to drop the gun. *CLICK.*

I fired my gun and the shit was not even loaded FML! He had his gun pointed at Ted's head.

"I'm taking you disloyal ass niggas out if that's the last thing I do," he said looking Ted in the eyes. I used Paco taking his eyes off me to my advantage and pulled the gun out that I had under the couch.

"You shoot me then your friend dies," Paco said to me feeling the heat from the gun that I had pointed at him.

"You think I give a fuck?" I said pointing my gun at Ted.

"Yo' fam, what you doing?" Ted asked with a shocked look on his face. "It's nothing personal, but business," I said before ending his life. Paco shot me in the thigh and I fired two shots hitting him in the chest. I limped over to him and shot him two more times before making my way out the house. I jumped in my with car leg hurting like a motherfucker and drove to my house.

***

"Yo, Tasha?!" I yelled, struggling to get to the couch. I was feeling weaker by the minute. I laid on the couch feeling real dizzy.

"What the fuck? What happened?" I heard her panicking.

"I got shot," I weakly answered her.

"Hello. I need an ambulance quick, he's been shot!!" I heard her yell into the phone before everything went black.

Chapter 21

Lala

I was on my break chatting with one of the nurses that worked in the emergency room when I seen a gurney with Stacks' friend rush by. My heart immediately started beating real fast and after calling Stacks ten times and getting no answer, I started thinking the worst.

"Jennifer, what's going on with that patient that was just rushed in?" I asked the ER's charge nurse.

"Who Kenneth Bell?" she asked, looking through a folder.

"The heavyset dude that resembles Rick Ross a little bit," I said not knowing Bear's real name.

"Yes, Kenneth. He suffered a gunshot wound to the femur. He lost a lot of blood and is unconscious at the moment. Is that a friend of yours?" she asked, writing notes in the chart she was looking in.

"A friend of my boyfriend, keep me posted ok?" I said quickly remembering that this was the same guy Lisa was dating. The dude from the party, that's where I remembered him from. *OMG, Lisa*; I thought as I picked up the phone to call her.

"Hey bestie!" she answered in a happy tone.

"Lisa I need you to come down to the hospital quick," I said not wanting to be the bearer of bad news.

"Why what happened? Is everything ok with the baby?" she asked me all in one breath.

"N-n-no, it's not the baby, it's, it's, it's Bear," I stuttered.

"What did you say? Bear? My Bear? What's wrong with him, Lala?" she asked on the verge of crying. I could tell that she really liked him. She even admitted to me that she loved him. She even planned on quitting her job at the club and going back to school. I loved how he changed her and made her see her worth. I wasn't ready for that to change.

"LALA!!!" she yelled diverting my attention back to the phone call. "CAN YOU TELL ME WHAT THE HELL IS GOING ON?!?" she barked in the phone.

"Lisa, just come down to the hospital please and I'll better explain to you ok?" I said, trying to calm her down a little.

"Ok," she sadly said before she hung up.

An hour later, Lisa and I were both sitting in the waiting room holding hands. Jennifer came towards us and we both stood up.

"Ok we were able to remove the bullet and stabilize him. He's in ICU now. We had to sedate him so that he can rest, but he should be up in a few hours," she said patting Lisa on the back.

"Thanks Jen," I said hugging her. While Lisa went to go sit by Bear's bedside, I stayed in the hallway and called Stacks for the 15th time. I was really starting to worry until I saw his name flash across my screen.

"Why haven't you been answering my calls?" I snapped.

"Relax ma, this is not a good time for me." I could hear the stress in his voice.

"What's wrong?" I asked, sitting down in one of the lobby chairs.

"My brother was just shot, one of my workers was found dead, and I cannot get a hold of Bear," he sighed. I thought of how I was going to break the news to him about his friend.

"Well um Anthony, Bear is here," I said hating that I had to deliver bad news to two people that I loved.

"Here where?" he asked, raising his voice a little.

"U-uh at the hospital I work. He was um rushed into here a few hours ago." I hesitated a little not sure how he was going to take the news.

"FUCK!" he yelled before hanging up the phone.

***

Once my shift was over, I went home to lay down. I called Lisa to check on her and she planned on staying at the hospital by Bear's side until he woke up. I filled the tub with warm water, poured some of my vanilla bean bubble bath in it, and grabbed my phone to text Stacks.

Me: *Are you ok?*

I got in the tub and laid back, until I heard my phone vibrate.

Bae: *I'm ok, how's my baby?*

Me: *Hungry.*

Even though he just filled the fridge with groceries I really wanted to see him. I wanted to fall asleep in his arms so bad.

Bae: *What do you want to eat?*

Me: *I want a big fat juicy burger, large seasoned fried and an extra large banana shake.* I replied.

Just thinking about the food made me really hungry.

Me: *Bring me a jar of pickles too!* I replied before putting my phone on the floor and laying back down to relax.

"Wake up ma?" I opened my eyes and saw Stacks standing there with a towel in his hand. I didn't even know I fell asleep in the water. He lifted my body out of the water and carried me over to the bed. He dried me off and grabbed my coconut cream body lotion off of the dresser. He gently rubbed my body with the lotion.

"Mmhhm," I moaned at how good he was with his hands. Once he was done, he told me to get dressed and come downstairs to eat. I walked down the stairs to a home cooked meal. *I must have been sleeping in the tub for a long time*; I thought.

"This is not what I asked for," I snapped. I was really craving that burger.

"You need to stop feeding my baby that bullshit!" he said placing a plate of loaded mash potatoes, steak, corn, and a chef salad in front of me. "Sit down and eat," he said as if I was a little child.

"Well did you at least bring me my pickles, I want to eat them with my ranch dip," I said pouring ranch all over my food. These days my craving for ranch was stronger than ever.

"It's on the counter," he said before climbing up the stairs and leaving me to eat alone.

After I was done eating, I grabbed my jar of pickles and ranch dip and headed up the stairs.

"The food was good," I said getting in the bed. He grabbed the jar and opened the pickles for me. "Thanks." I watched him text somebody on the phone.

"Who are you texting Anthony?" I jealously asked.

"When you decided to be sneaky and shit you lost all your rights over me, you can't ask me shit," he said, putting his phone on the dresser and reaching for the remote.

"Whatever," I answered while eating my pickles. I got up to put the jar in the fridge and brushed my teeth. I got back in bed and Stacks was laying there stripped down to his boxers. His sexy ass knew what he was doing.

"I'm going to Columbia for a week," he said as soon as I got under the comforter.

"Why?" I asked trying to get comfortable.

"My brother was airlifted there to get better treatment, so I'm going to be by his side. He's in a coma now, but we have faith that he will wake up." He looked at a picture of him and me that sat on the nightstand.

"He's going to be ok," I assured him. He grabbed me by my waist and pulled my close to him. My body automatically responded to his touch. I turned around so that I was facing him and gave him a kiss on the lips.

"Stop Lala," he told me as he looked me in the eyes.

"Why?" I was on verge of tears.

"I can't do this with you. I gave you my heart and you broke it. You played me like I was some dumb nigga. I'm done with you." He clenched his jaw ad he shattered my heart.

"Then why are you here?" I asked as the tears started to fall. He didn't respond to me and he rubbed my belly.

"My grandmother is coming down to be with you while I'm gone," he said.

"Why I don't need a babysitter, I'm a grown ass woman?"

"That's not up for discussion. I don't want you here alone." I rolled my eyes and just laid there.

"If you're only here for the baby, you can leave! I can get rid of it, so that you have no reason to feel obligated to be by my side," I spoke those words, but I didn't mean it. There was no way in hell I was going to abort my child. I just wanted him to feel the hurt that I was feeling.

"Don't fuck with me Lala, I will kill you if you even think about calling an abortion clinic," he said, grabbing my face. "Do you fucking hear me!?" he yelled in my face.

"Yes!" We were supposed to be happy together, but because I screwed up I was forced to be a single mother.

"What I told you about stressing my baby?" He held me tighter.

"You don't care about me no more," I cried.

"I love you, Lala," he confessed while closing his eyes.

"Then why don't you want to be with me?" I asked sounding like a little girl.

"I did, but you fucked up."

"I know, but baby I'm sorry. Give us a chance to be a family. Please?" I begged.

"Shh. Go to sleep," he said before he dozed off.

His phone started ringing and curiosity got the best of me, so I got up and took the phone with me to the bathroom. I closed the door, sat on the toilet, and with trembling fingers unlocked his phone. I saw a few messages from his brother, dad, grandma, but then an unknown number caught my attention. Before I could open the message, the phone was snatched out of my hand.

"Why the fuck are you going through my phone, Lala?!" Stacks asked with a frown on his face.

"If you wasn't pregnant, I swear I would fuck you up for being so dumb!" He walked out of the bathroom leaving me with my thoughts.

Chapter 22

James

I've been lurking and finally studying that nigga and it was almost that time to attack. The cash flow was coming through, but not as much as it was before. I knew exactly what I had to do to get that back. It hurt my soul to find out my bitch was pregnant by that nigga, but I had something for that ass.

I had no intentions on hurting Lala. I just had to get rid of that nigga so things could go back to the way it used to be. I was at Ashley's house packing my things. Although she was carrying child, I did not want her to think for a second that we was going to be together.

"Where you going?" she asked walking into the room. She went out to lunch with Loye and I was hoping to get all my things out before she came home.

"I'm going back home," I told her as I packed.

"Home. Where?" She placed her hands on her hips. I could see the little bulge in her belly making me feel bad for leaving. My heart was with Lala and I was not going to stay where I didn't want to be. The grass on the other side wasn't greener. I learned my lesson and was ready to go back home to my baby.

"My home, the one I built with Lala."

"Lala?" she said laughing.

"Lala is at her HOME with the nigga she's pregnant by. She is not worried about you! Your home is here with me and this baby James!" she yelled in my face.

"Fuck you, Ashley, the only time I want to deal with you is if it's in regards to my child. I want nothing else to do with you. It's a wrap!" I said grabbing my bags and bringing it to my car.

"You a dumb nigga! How the fuck you going to leave your family for a bitch that has her own. Get it through your fucking head, LALA IS OVER YOU!"

WHAM!

I backhanded the bitch, did she forgot who the fuck I was? Yeah part of what she said was true. I knew that Lala wasn't going to come back home willingly. But, with her baby daddy dead she would have no choice, but to come crawling back. When she did, I was going to accept her and that baby with open arms. Before I could get that done, I had to kill that nigga. I called up Rico. Murder was on my mind and Stacks was my victim.

Chapter 23

Ashley

The nerve of that nigga. I was the one pregnant with his child and he wanted to tell me that he was leaving me for Lala. Over my dead body! I had to get rid of this bitch once and for all. I thought about letting her live because Ted was dead, Bear was in the hospital, and she was pregnant. But no, that was not enough.

Even though she was in her own relationship, she still had to have my man. I quickly dressed in a pair of all black sweats, a hoodie, and a pair of all black Air Force Ones. I pulled the red wig over my head, put on a black hat, and threw my shades on. I picked up the bag of money that I sat on the foot of the bed and left the house. It was time to get rid of this bitch.

Sitting in my car waiting for my problem solver, my phone started to ring.

"Hello?" I answered.

"Did you get rid of the baby yet?" the caller asked.

"No, not yet," I said, looking out the window. I looked down at my watch; it was 8:47 p.m.. The guy I was supposed to meet with was running late.

"Well, when are you going to get it done?" I was beyond annoyed with this phone call, so I decided to cut it short.

"Listen, I'm going to get rid of the baby soon! Don't worry, word will never got out that it's your baby in me!!" I yelled, ending the phone call.

I sat in my car for another hour before I heard a tap on my window. "You got all my money?" he asked as soon as I rolled down the window.

"Yes it's all in the bag. I want this done soon! I'm so sick of this bitch." He stared at the picture of Lala that I handed to him. He looked back at me for a minute, then grabbed the money, and was off. He was a weird ass nigga if you asked me, but anything to get Lala out of James and I lives was what I was willing to do.

I just hoped he would hurry up and get rid of her, so that I could do the same with this baby. I was tired of this nigga calling me. I paid him $15,000 for his sperm and signed an agreement that the child would be terminated. As if I wanted to let his little demon grow in me, yeah right.

Looking at myself in my review mirror, I smiled. I was finally going to get the happily ever after that I deserved. James was finally going to be all mines. My threat Lala would no longer be an issue anymore. I put the key in the ignition and started the car.

My car was instantly filled with sounds of Young Dro's song *Fuck that bitch* and that was exactly what I thought as I drove off. FUCK THAT BITCH!

Chapter 24

Tasha

I listened behind the door as Bear and this chick talked. I was beyond pissed! He told me not to come visit him, so that I wouldn't risk running into Stacks, but the real reason he didn't want me around was because he was booed up with this bitch. I put up with a lot of Bear's BS. I was his true ride or die, but he seemed to have forgotten that.

I knew exactly what I had to do to make sure that this bitch was out the picture. If I carried out with the plan and hit the lick on Stacks then we could disappear. I was all in for it and I was going to do whatever it took to make sure my man and I made it to the private island. I was in too deep just to sit back and let the next chick take my spot. Oh no!! That was not going to happen.

"I love you, Bear." My heart literally stopped beating. I pinched myself just to make sure I wasn't dreaming. I wanted to go into that room and snatch that trick by her weave. How dare she tell my man that she loved him? I held my breath waiting for Bear's reply. When he told her that he loved her, too, I told myself that it was all apart of the plan, but my women's intuition told me otherwise.

Trying to hold back my tears, I ran out of the hospital to my car. Once I got inside my car, I broke down crying. How could he do this to me? My pain instantly turned into anger as I made a phone call to finally get things over with once and for all.

"We on for tonight," I said as soon as my partner in crime answered the phone.

"No doubt, pick me up around 11 p.m," the person on the other line responded. We went over our plan, until we had it down pack before we ended the call. I was going to finish up the plan and make Bear proud of me. He'd be so happy that I was able to pull this off that he would have no choice but to make me his wife. Wife? Yeah, I liked the sound of that.

Chapter 25

Bear

I couldn't fucking believe how things went! To say I was pissed was an understatement. What made the situation worse was that I wasn't for sure if that nigga Paco was dead or not. The only thing I was able to get out of Lisa was that Stacks was suppose to be going to Columbia to be with his family. I asked her where Lala would be and she told me home with his grandma. This was perfect.

Now all I had to do was get the fuck out of this hospital, so that I could do what I had to do. If Paco was still alive then chances are that he was going to tell Stacks about me. So my best bet was to get what I could and get ghost. I was still mad that I wouldn't be able to kill him, but hey, I'd settle for hurting him in the worst way.

"I sent one of my homies a text and watched Lisa pay attention to one of her reality shows. I really did feel something for her, I didn't know if it was love or lust, but something was there. I wanted to be with her and explore where this could go, but I knew that was impossible.

I knew she did not want to relocate from her best friend and her life, plus the chances of Tasha sitting back and letting that happen wasn't likely. I felt like Tasha could be the end of me, she knew too much information that she posed as a threat. I would have to kill her in order to get rid of her, but Tasha was in a way my ride or die so me killing her was not going to happen.

I didn't know whether I owed Lisa an explanation or should I just disappear. I knew she was going to be hurt since she told me how much she loved me, but hey what could I do? I didn't tell her to fall for me. She should have pocketed her feelings. She was a pretty girl; she'd get over me. I planned on releasing myself tonight after she went home to avoid having to say goodbye or explaining myself.

"Come climb in bed and let daddy slide up in that," I said rubbing my hands up and down her bare thigh.

"Bae, we're in a hospital," she said looking at me like I was crazy.

"So, go lock that door and jump on this dick." I pulled her down to me for a kiss. If this was my last time seeing her, I wanted to bury my wood deep in them guts. I planned on fucking her in every position that I could think of. This was that goodbye dick she was going to get. Like the good bitch she was, she got up and locked the door. "Come climb on my face, a nigga hungry," I said pulling out my dick and stroking it. She undid her shorts, and squatted over my face. Her wetness dripped in my mouth as I ate her out with everything in me.

Chapter 26

Lisa

I felt myself falling deeper and deeper for Bear, and at this point I didn't care. I finally had a man that loved me for me. He complimented me, he stimulated my mind, and he pushed me to see what Lala had been trying to show me. I was too pretty to be stripping in a club. I had more to offer myself. It took me meeting the right man to figure it out. Now, that I had him, I couldn't fathom the thought of having to live without him.

The way he put it on me let me know that he loved me. I never had a man make love to me with so much passion. He was going to be released from the hospital in two days and I was already preparing things for him to come home with me.

After a few hours of laying in my man's arms, it was time for me to go home. I couldn't wait until the morning so that I could be here bright eyed and bushy tail by my man's bedside. While walking to my car, I kept getting a feeling that something wasn't right. I pulled out my gun and held it next to me for protection. A bitch was going to get returned back to their sender for fucking with me tonight.

Once I approached my car, I was pissed. Somebody busted all of my windows and painted home wrecker all over my car. I noticed something in my driver's seat, so I opened the door. My jaw dropped to the ground; there was a black dress and matching black heels laid on the seat.

VROOM! Was all I heard and as soon as I looked up it was too late. Somebody was driving towards me full speed. I tried to lift my gun and tried shooting at the on coming vehicle, but I wasn't quick enough. The force of the car slamming against my body sent me flying across the parking lot. I tried to open my eyes, but they were too heavy.

Lord forgive me for all my sins, please watch over Lala, my godchild, and Bear. I love you Bear.......

Chapter 27

Lala

"You sure you be ok?" Stacks grandma asked me as I dropped her off at the airport. She had to fly back to Flint to check on her husband who had a stroke.

"Yes Nana, I will be ok. Go home and take care of Papa," I said giving her a hug. I sat in my car and watched as she disappeared through the doors of the airport.

Pulling out of the parking lot, I made my way to Wendy's. I had a taste for a chili-baked potato with extra cheese and sour cream.

"Welcome to Wendy's, can I take you order?" the lady spoke through the drive thru speaker. I could tell she was ghetto by the way she was smacking that gum.

"Yes, may I please have two chili baked potatoes, add broccoli and extra cheese to both please. Add a large fry and a large strawberry lemonade." I gave her my order while posting pictures of my recent sonogram on IG.

"Will that be all?" Ghetto Fabulous asked me.

"Yes!" I said driving up to the second window. I handed her Stacks debit card and waited for my food.

As I was driving home, I had a feeling that someone was following me. I shrugged it off and just thought that I was being paranoid. I parked my car in the driveway, grabbed my phone, food, and went inside. I made sure the doors were locked and that the security alarm was on. I got comfy on the floor and got ready to dig into my food until I was interrupted by my phone ringing.

"Hello?!" I answered annoyed. This damn caller was messing with my food and I did not play about eating.

"What did you buy from Wendy's?" Stacks asked shocking the hell out of me. I should of checked the caller I.D before hitting the answer button on my Bluetooth. "What did I tell you about feeding my baby that garbage!" he yelled in my ear not waiting on a response.

"It's only a baked potato gosh! I'm supposed to satisfy my cravings you know," I said, rolling my eyes.

"Did Nana catch her flight?" he asked, changing the subject.

"Yes," I answered with a mouth full of food.

"I'll be home in the morning. Go feed my baby and call me before you go to bed. Make sure the doors are locked and the alarm is on," he ordered.

"Yes daddy," I replied still going in on my food. I just wished he'd hang up already, so I could eat in peace.

After eating and showering, I called Stacks to let him know I was getting ready to go to sleep. We talked on the phone for hours like high school lovers. Hopefully when he came home, he was going to consider getting back together. I decided to hang up after listening to him snore for 10 minutes. I really did love Stacks.

It took me going through a bad man to appreciate the good man that I had. I thanked James everyday for fucking up and allowing me to meet my true soul mate. I called Lisa a few times and got her voicemail.

"Hey I know you're probably with Bear, but I was wondering if you wanted to go shopping tomorrow. Call me when you get a chance. Love you bestie, bye." I left her a voicemail, said my prayers and snuggled up in bed. I wasn't big on praying, but since I met Stacks, he expressed how important it was to have a relationship with God.

***

BANG! BANG! BANG! BANG!

"Somebody help me please!!" I thought I was dreaming, but when the banging and cries got louder, I went to the door. I looked out the peephole and saw a girl cradling a baby crying. Being the good Samaritan that I was, I opened the door. "Oh, my God, are you ok?!" I asked stepping outside.

Before I realized the baby was a doll and this was a set up, it was too late. Strong arms grabbed me from behind and put a rag up to my nose. *Lord please watch over my baby and I, please protect us from any harm, and please be with us.* I prayed before I passed out.

Chapter 28

Stacks

"Tio vas a jugar conmigo? *(Tio going to play with me)?*" my niece asked jumping on my bed.

"Hoy no tengo que volver a casa," I responded to her, kissing her plump cheeks. I loved my niece and I couldn't wait to be a father myself. I grabbed my phone to call Lala, but got no answer. I decided to let her and the baby get some rest, so I sent her a text telling her to call me as soon as she wakes up.

My brother was still in a coma, but he was doing better. Last night, I saw him wiggle his fingers, so it was only a matter of time. I really wanted to get to the bottom of this. My gut was telling me that this wasn't James. My father always told me in the game you have to trust your gut instinct. So now I had to find the snake that was lurking in my grass.

"Come sit with me before you leave my son," my pops said to me as I walked down the stairs with my suitcase. I was in no rush since I was taking his private plane home. I sat in one of the chairs across from him. "So what are you going to do?" he asked me pouring himself a glass of orange juice.

"I'm on top of everything, the niggas that did this to Paco will pay," I said eating my Changua.

"No, no, no. I know you will handle that. I mean that young lady you have pregnant with my grandchild," he said eating some of his food.

"I am going to take care of my child like a man pops," I replied, pouring myself some juice.

"Anthony, everyone makes mistakes and they deserve second chances. The same way you put Donna through locura she gave you a dose of your medicine. I could tell that you love her and she loves you. This is your second chance, don't let it pass you by because of your pride," he said, lecturing me. I listened to his words and allowed it to marinate in my mind.

He snapped his fingers and a maid walked up to him holding a velvet box. He took the box and slid it across the table to me. I picked it up and opened it. I had to close it and prepared my eyes for a second look. Inside was a pink rectangular diamond ring. The diamonds on that bad boy was shining bright damn near blinding a nigga. The weight of the ring let me know that pops spent mad dough on it.

"True love only comes around once, but you got a second chance. Do the right thing," he said before getting up and leaving me to my thoughts. He was right. Yeah, Lala fucked up one time, but who hasn't. When I got back home, we really had to talk about things to see if this was what she really wanted and if so she'd be my wife.

***

As soon as my flight landed, I decided to go check on Bear. I had to really talk to him and ask him what was really good, there was a snake and I was determined to behead that motherfucker. I called Lala again, but got no answer. I texted her telling her to get ready so that we could go out.

"Are you looking for Kenneth?" the nurse asked as she read the confused look on my face. I was standing in his room, but it was empty.

"Yes, did they transfer him to another room?" I asked.

"No, he actually checked himself out last night," she replied.

"Thanks," I said, walking out of the hospital. A bad feeling suddenly rushed me as I made my way home.

Parking behind Lala's car, I walked to the front door. It was closed, but unlocked. I was pissed. She knew better than to leave the damn door unlocked.

"Lala! Why the fuck is the damn door unlocked?" I yelled through the house as I walked up the stairs. The bed was unmade and her phone was on the nightstand. "Lala!!" I called out for her walking through every room in the house and still nothing.

My heart started beating fast that if someone was standing next to me they could have heard it. I made my way to the kitchen and saw a box and a note on the counter. I opened the box and saw a prepaid phone, and then I picked up the note and began to read it.

My knees started to get weak and I could feel myself get lightheaded. I went over to the sink to wash my face.

Maybe my eyes were playing tricks on me. This could not be real. I dried my face and picked the note up again.

We have your bitch and if you want her and your kid alive, you'll do as we say. Stay close to the phone and we'll be in contact soon. The words haunted me as I read them over and over again. This couldn't be fucking happening to me again!!

Lord, I know I'm a sinner and I do not deserve to be blessed; however, I'm begging you for a miracle right now. Please give me the strength to bring my wife and child home safely. Amen.

I sat at the table feeling my heartbreak. Why was this happening to me again? All I could think about was Donna and how broken I was having to bury her and my kids. The thought of having to bury Lala and my unborn was a hard pill to swallow. I took a look at the baby's sonogram Lala had framed in an 'I love you daddy' picture frame.

BRRINNG!! The ringing of the prepaid phone brought me back to this deja vu I was experiencing again. I cleared my throat and answered the phone.

"Hello?"

TO BE CONTINUED......

Author's Bio

Lucinda John is 21 years old and resides in Fort Lauderdale, Fl. She is the mother of three kids and in her spare time she loves to read. She started writing in middle school and after reading and supporting so many authors, she decided it was time that she put her gift to use. Lucinda is a very open, happy, loving, and caring person. She is currently working on more projects that will be released soon.

Text Shan to 22828 to stay up to date with new releases, sneak peeks, and more from Shan and the ladies of Shan Presents

CPSIA information can be obtained
at www.ICGtesting.com
Printed in the USA
LVOW02s0021070617
537193LV00009B/135/P